D1589910

BIGGLES OF THE
FIGHTER SQUADRON

'I must be crazy!' he told himself angrily, coming to his senses with a rush, and raced back towards the Lines. A Fokker D.VII appeared from nowhere, and he grabbed his gun-lever. Rat-tat! Two shots flashed out, that was all. Furiously he struck the cocking-handles of the guns to clear the supposed jam. And then he tried them again. Nothing happened, and he knew that he had run through all his ammunition!

BIGGLES BOOKS PUBLISHED IN THIS EDITION:

Biggles: The Camels are Coming
Biggles in France
Biggles Learns to Fly
Biggles and the Rescue Flight
Biggles Flies East
Biggles of the Fighter Squadron
Biggles: The Cruise of the Condor
Biggles & Co.
Biggles in Spain
Biggles and the Secret Mission
Biggles Defies the Swastika
Biggles Fails to Return
Biggles Delivers the Goods
Biggles Defends the Desert
Biggles in the Orient
Biggles – Flying Detective
Biggles: Spitfire Parade (a graphic novel)

Biggles adventures available
on cassette from Tellastory,
featuring Tim Pigott-Smith as Biggles:

Biggles Learns to Fly
Biggles Flies East
Biggles Defies the Swastika
Biggles in Spain
Biggles – Flying Detective
Biggles and the Secret Mission

BIGGLES OF THE FIGHTER SQUADRON

CAPTAIN W. E. JOHNS

RED FOX

Red Fox would like to express their grateful thanks for help given in preparing these new editions to Jennifer Schofield, author of *By Jove, Biggles*, Linda Shaughnessy of A. P. Watt Ltd and especially to John Trendler, editor of *Biggles & Co*, the quarterly magazine for Biggles enthusiasts.

A Red Fox Book
Published by Random House Children's Books
20 Vauxhall Bridge Road, London SW1V 2SA

A division of Random House UK Ltd
London Melbourne Sydney Auckland
Johannesburg and agencies throughout the world

First published with the title
'Biggles of the Camel Squadron'
by John Hamilton 1934

Red Fox edition 1992

4 6 8 10 9 7 5 3

Set in 10.5/12pt Baskerville
Phototypeset by Intype, London

Printed and bound in Great Britain by
Cox & Wyman Ltd, Reading, Berkshire

RANDOM HOUSE UK Limited Reg. No. 954009

ISBN 0 09 921701 5

Contents

Foreword

Flight-Lieutenant Bigglesworth, R.F.C., known to his friends as 'Biggles', is a character well known to those who read *Popular Flying**. Some of his war-time exploits have already been published in book form under the title *The Camels Are Coming***.

Biggles is not entirely a fictitious character. True, he did not exist, as far as I am aware, under that name, but the exploits with which he has been credited have nearly all been built on a foundation of truth, although, needless to say, they were not all the efforts of a single individual. Students of air-war history may have no difficulty in recognising the actual incidents, and the name of the officers associated with them, although they are now presented in fiction form.

Sceptics may doubt this. Let them. The old saying about truth being stranger than fiction was never more apposite than in war flying, and I have hesitated to record some of the events which came under my personal notice for that very reason. I would not dare to 'arrange' a collision between an aeroplane and a kite balloon, and allow the hero to survive. Yet Willy Coppens, the Belgian Ace, did just that, and is alive to-day to tell us about it.

* Aviation magazine which ran from 1932–1939, which W. E. Johns edited. The first Biggles stories appeared in this magazine.
** The first Biggles book, containing all the early Biggles adventures that appeared in *Popular Flying*. Reissued by Red Fox as *Biggles in The Camels are Coming*.

Again, I should blush to dress my hero, after he had been forced to land on the wrong side of the lines, in a girl's clothes, and allow him to be pestered with the unwelcome attentions of German officers for weeks before making his escape. The officer who resorted to that romantic method of escape is now in business in London. And yet again, what author would dare to make his hero slide down the cable of a captive kite balloon, to the ground, without being killed? Yet it happened, and I have heard the story from the officer's own lips, and seen his hands that still bear the marks of that grim adventure. A photograph is still extant of the machine that rammed an eight-hundred-foot wireless pylon. The pilot was rendered unconscious in the crash, and the machine remained transfixed in the pylon, hundreds of feet above the ground. Of all amazing aeroplane crashes that surely holds the palm. It is almost incredible that the pilot survived, but he did.

I merely mention these facts to demonstrate to those unfamiliar with war flying history what amazing things could, and did, happen, things far more strange than those recorded in this book, which—and I say this in order that there should be no misunderstanding on the point—has been written more for the entertainment of the younger generation than the hard-baked warrior.

Technical expressions have therefore been avoided as far as possible, and the stories told in a form which I hope everyone will be able to understand.

Finally, I hope—and I say this in all sincerity—that something may be learned from the 'combat tactics' employed by Biggles and his friends, by those who may one day find themselves in the cockpit of a fighting aeroplane, carrying on the glorious tradition of the Flying Service.

Lingfield
1934

W.E.J.

The word 'Hun' used in this book was the generic term for anything belonging to the German enemy. It was used in a familiar sense, rather than derogatory. Witness the fact that in the R.F.C. a hun was also a pupil at a flying training school.

W.E.J.

Chapter 1
The Professor

A slight fall of snow during the night had covered the aerodrome of Squadron No. 266, R.F.C.*, with a thin white mantle, and a low-hanging canopy of indigo-tinted cloud, stretching from horizon to horizon, held a promise of more to come.

Captain Bigglesworth, from the window of the officers' mess**, contemplated the wintry scene for the tenth time with bored impatience, then turned to the group of officers who were gathered around the mess fire discussing such matters of professional interest as machine-guns, bullets, and shooting generally.

'You say what you like, Mac,' Biggles interrupted MacLaren, the popular flight-commander of B Flight, 'but I am absolutely certain that not one pilot in a thousand allows enough deflection when he is shooting. Look at any machine you like after a "dog-fight***", and you will find nearly all the bullet-holes are behind the ring markings. The same thing happens if you've been trench strafing.

'If you look over the side, you can see a hundred Germans shooting at you with any old weapon they've been able to grab—machine-guns, rifles, revolvers, and

* Royal Flying Corps 1914–1918. An Army Corps responsible for military aeronautics. Renamed the Royal Air Force (RAF) when amalgamated with the Royal Naval Air Service 1st April 1918.
** The place where officers eat their meals and relax together.
*** An aerial battle.

all the rest of it. But where do the bullets go? I don't know. But I'll bet you anything you like they're miles behind. Not one in a thousand touches the machine, anyway. And why? Because it takes a lot of imagination to shoot five hundred feet in front of your target and expect to hit it.

'You don't expect the infantry to sit down and work out by mathematics the fact that you are travelling about two hundred feet a second, and that by the time his bullet reaches the place where the machine was when he pulled the trigger the machine is no longer there. And it's the same with archie*. Watch a machine in the sky being shelled. Where is all the smoke? In nine cases out of ten it's about half a mile behind.

'Every now and then you get a gunner who knows his stuff; but a lot of them don't. Look at it this way. Suppose you are diving at a hundred and fifty miles an hour at twenty thousand feet up. A hundred and fifty miles an hour is over two hundred feet a second. It takes about twenty seconds for a shell to reach twenty thousand feet, so if the gunner aims at the machine without allowing deflection, the machine is about a mile away when the shell bursts!' he concluded emphatically.

'It's purely a matter of mathematics,' said a quiet voice near at hand.

Biggles started, and all eyes turned towards the speaker, a small, round-faced youth who was reclining in a cane chair. He nodded solemnly as he realised that everyone was looking at him.

'Did you say something?' said Biggles, with a questioning stare.

'I said that deflection shooting was, in my opinion,

* Slang: anti-aircraft gunfire.

12

purely a matter of mathematics,' replied the youth, blinking owlishly.

A bellow of laughter split the air, for Henry Watkins, the speaker, had joined the squadron in France direct from a flying training school about one hour earlier, and these were the first words he had been heard to utter.

'What makes you think so, laddie?' asked Biggles, with a wink at MacLaren, when the mirth had subsided.

'Well, I have analysed this very desideratum—theoretically, of course,' confessed Henry, 'and I long ago reached the conclusion that Euclidian precision with a machine-gun can be determined by a simple mathematical, or I should say algebraical, formula.'

'Is that so? And you are going to do sums in the air before you start shooting, eh?' grinned Biggles.

'Why not?' returned Henry quickly. 'Mental arithmetic is always fascinating, and logarithms will lick luck every time. I have evolved a pet theory of my own which will probably revolutionise the whole art of aerial combat, and I am anxious to test it in practice at the first available opportunity.'

'That's fine. Well, you won't have long to wait!' interposed Biggles grimly. 'You'll get your chance just as soon as this muck lifts!' He indicated the clouds with an upward sweep of his thumb.

'Good!' replied Henry calmly. 'Perhaps you would like me to show you my idea. Now, for the sake of example, let us assume that a hostile aircraft, or Hun, if you prefer the common colloquialism, is proceeding along a path of flight which we will call A—B, banking at an angle of, shall we say, thirty degrees—so. These two coffee-cups will indicate the imaginary line,' he

13

went on, arranging the two cups on a card-table in front of the fire.

'Now, I am approaching in my Camel plane on a course which we will call C—D—two more cups, thanks!—at an angle of bank of sixty degrees. Now, by a combination of factors which I will presently explain, I will demonstrate to you that a prolongation of the muzzles of my Vickers guns will intercept the geometrical arc A—C in X seconds plus the cube root of the square of the chord B—C—a very simple equation. Now, if I equal Y—'

'Why?' broke in Biggles, in a dazed voice.

'Yes, I said Y—'

'I mean, what for?' Biggles demanded.

'Well, call me Z if you like; it's all the same.'

'Hold hard—hold hard!' cried Biggles. 'What's all this about? What is all this XYZ stuff, anyway? I'm not a blinking triangle! You can be the whole blooming alphabet if you like, as far as I am concerned, and if you think you can knock Huns down by drawing imaginary lines, you go ahead!'

'Well, there it is, and that's all there is to it,' said Henry, with a shrug of resignation. 'The whole thing is purely a matter of mathematics!'

'Mathematics, my eye! If you start working out sums on my patrol I'll show you a new line of flight with the cube root of my foot when we get back on the ground!' promised Biggles, scowling.

The door opened, and Major Mullen, the C.O.*, entered.

'This stuff is not going to lift, I'm afraid!' he said, nodding towards the window. 'But we shall have to

* Commanding officer.

14

try to put up a show of some sort or other, or wing headquarters will start a scream. What about dropping a few Cooper bombs* on a Jerry** aerodrome—Aerodrome No. 32, for instance—eh, Bigglesworth?'

'Good enough, sir! That suits me,' replied Biggles. 'Anything for a quiet life. I'll go crazy if I loaf about here toasting in front of the fire much longer!'

Henry sprang to his feet and started off towards the door.

'Hi, where do you think you're off to?' called Biggles.

'I thought I was going to bomb Aerodrome No. 32. Am I not coming with you?' cried Henry, in dismay.

'You! I should say so! Sit down, and don't be silly!' growled Biggles. 'You'd be lost to the world in five minutes if you got into that soup. You get a pencil and paper and go on working out your sums!'

'Lost? Absurd!' snorted Henry. 'With a good compass it is impossible to get lost. Cloud flying is purely a matter of mathematics.'

Major Mullen smiled.

'Who told you that?' he asked, in surprise.

'Don't you start him off on that ABC stuff again, sir,' protested Biggles quickly. 'He reckons he's going to shoot Huns down by algebra.' He turned to Henry. 'Look here, kid,' he said, 'I don't want to discourage you, but do you think you could keep me in sight if I let you come with me?'

'Keep you in sight?' echoed Henry. 'Of course I could!'

'By mathematics, I suppose?'

'Certainly!'

* Small bombs weighing around 20lb, filled with high explosive.
** Slang: German.

15

'All right, Professor. But you leave your copy-book and pencil at home, and keep your eye on me. If you lose me in the fog, don't sit around doing mental arithmetic, trying to work out where I am by your XYZ stuff. You come home—quick, or you might run into somebody who draws lines—not imaginary ones, either—with Spandau* guns. Come on, then. Come on, Algy. Three'll be enough.'

Ten minutes later they took off in a swirl of snow, and, climbing swiftly, soon reached the gloom of the cloud-bank. At four thousand feet Biggles burst out at the top into brilliant sunshine, with a suddenness that was startling, and looked around quickly for the other two Camels**. Algy emerged from the opaque vapour about fifty yards away, and instantly took up his position close to Biggles' right wing-tip. But of Henry there was no sign.

Biggles circled for a few minutes, grumbling at the delay, then spied the missing Camel among the cloud-tops about a mile away, heading on a course at forty-five degrees to his own. He raced after it, but just as he reached it, the Camel once more disappeared into the cold grey mist. He muttered an exclamation of annoyance as he pulled up to avoid a collision. 'Working out his blinking sums, I expect,' he mused.

Presently the Camel appeared again, far to the east, still heading out over hostile country. Biggles ground his teeth and let him go. He could not have caught him

* German machine guns were often referred to as Spandaus due to the fact that many were manufactured at Spandau, Germany.
** Sopwith Camel, a single-seater biplane fighter with twin machine guns synchronised to fire through the propeller. Tricky to fly. See front cover for illustration.

16

up, anyway. He made a despairing gesture to Algy in the other Camel, and then, turning, they sped away together towards the objective aerodrome.

For some minutes they held on their course, then a strong Albatros* patrol came into view, sailing serenely through the blue sky at a tremendous height. It was heading farther in over its own Lines**. But Biggles kept a watchful eye on it, prepared to dive into the clouds for safety at the first indication that they had been seen.

Presently the black-crossed enemy machines started diving down, and disappeared into the mist some distance ahead. For another quarter of an hour Biggles and Algy cruised along just above the cloud-tops, keeping a wary eye on the sky, ready to dive for the cover the clouds would provide, should the Albatroses reappear.

'We should be there, or thereabouts,' Biggles decided at last, glancing at his watch and then at his compass. With a warning wave to Algy, he throttled back and glided steadily downwards through the grey mist. Not until he was at less than five hundred feet was he clear of the clouds, and he examined the gloomy earth below anxiously.

So dark was it after the brilliant sunshine above that for a moment or two he could not see anything. Then he saw Algy, a hundred yards away, rock his wings violently, turn to the right, and plunge down, with a line of glittering tracer bullets*** leaping from his guns.

Biggles swung his Camel round in its own length and

* German single-seater fighter with two fixed machine guns.
** The front line trenches where the opposing armies faced one another.
*** Phosphorus-loaded bullets whose course through the air could be seen by day or by night.

17

tore down after him, leaning well over the left side of his cockpit to see what Algy was shooting at. A quiver of excitement ran through him, and a grunt of surprise escaped his lips. They had emerged from the clouds almost immediately over the enemy aerodrome. But it was not that which caused him to stiffen, every nerve tense, and crouch low in the cockpit.

On the aerodrome, taxi-ing towards the sheds, were a dozen Albatroses, evidently the high patrol they had seen in the air, and which had just landed. It was at once evident that the two Camels had been seen, for pandemonium reigned on the ground. Several groups of grey-clad German troops were racing towards what Biggles rightly assumed to be mobile machine-guns.

Several pilots jumped out of their machines and flung themselves on the ground, with their arms over their heads as the tracer bullets from the Vickers guns* started tearing up the turf around them. Two Albatroses tried to turn up-wind to take off, and collided with a crash that Biggles could hear above the noise of his engine.

Another black-crossed machine was whirling a blinding cloud of snow over a group of mechanics as it tore across the aerodrome on a down-wind take-off.

Biggles saw the first of Algy's bombs explode on the tarmac**, and the second within ten feet of a blue Albatros, smothering it with a shower of debris. With a grin on his face, he turned to pick out his own target.

Straight along the line of hangars he flew, working the bomb-toggle*** rhythmically until the eight 20-lb

---

* Machine guns firing a continuous stream of bullets at one squeeze of the trigger.
** The paved area in front of the hangars.
*** The bomb release handle.

18

Cooper bombs had left their racks. At the end of the sheds he whirled the Camel round in its own length, and, pointing his nose down at the still taxi-ing machines, he sprayed them with a shower of lead. The hangars* were in flames, blazing furiously in two or three places.

Several figures were prone on the ground, and Algy was busy scattering another group with his guns. A third Albatros had become entangled with the two that had collided, and Biggles raked all three of them with a stream of bullets. Two of the pilots leaped from their cockpits and sprinted out of the withering blast. Clouds of smoke from the fires and bombs drifted across the scene of destruction and rose upwards to the cloudbank, which reflected the orange glow of the inferno below.

'I think that'll about do,' thought Biggles. 'We've certainly given 'em a very warm time. Pity that ass Henry got lost, though. He'd have made things very much warmer still!' He sprayed the tarmac with a final burst, and then, waving joyously to Algy, pulled up in a steep zoom into the opaque mist.

Bursting out into the sunlight, he swerved violently to avoid colliding with a green-striped Albatros—evidently the one that had succeeded in taking off downwind—and he had perforated its wooden fuselage with a neat row of bullet-holes before the pilot recovered from his surprise.

Algy, emerging from the cloud-bank a few yards away, pumped a stream of bullets into the black-crossed machine** from the other side as it slowly turned

---

* Structure for housing aircraft.
** In the First World War, the German symbol was a Maltese cross—see front cover for illustration.

19

over on its back and plunged out of sight into the fog.

Side by side the two Camels sped back towards the Lines, the pilots waving to each other from time to time out of sheer lightheartedness.

Meanwhile, Henry was not having such a happy time. Somehow or other his carefully prepared plans were not panning out as he had fondly imagined they would. His trouble started early—in fact, from the very moment that he lost sight of his companions in the clammy, impenetrable fog.

After the first shock of discovery that he could no longer see his leader, he fixed his eyes on the instrument board and prepared to keep the machine on its course until he had climbed above the snow-cloud. But he quickly discovered this was not so easy as a careful study of his *Flying Training Manual* had led him to believe.

In spite of his efforts to prevent it, the compass needle jerked about all over the place, and he soon gave it up as hopeless and concentrated his attention on the inclinometer* in an endeavour to keep the machine on even keel. This again was far more difficult than he expected, for the bubble swung continually from one side to the other. The monotonous rush of the mist swirling past his cockpit began to make him feel dizzy, and he prayed fervently that he would not collide with one of the other two machines which he never doubted were flying alongside, although he could not see them.

Steering an erratic course, he at last broke through

* An instrument similar to a spirit level for showing the angle of the aircraft relative to the ground.

the surface of the fog, like a whale coming up for air, and looked around eagerly for the other machines. They were nowhere in sight. His jaw sagged foolishly, and he steered in turn at the four points of the compass, in comical consternation. A terrible feeling of loneliness gripped him as he slowly realised that he was alone in the sky.

He got out his map and with some difficulty worked out a compass course to the German aerodrome, confident that he would find the other machines there. He flew along with a worried frown on his face, looking for a possible enemy or the other two Camels.

He had just made a mental note that the dangers of war flying had been grossly exaggerated by the other pilots who had spoken to him about it, when a strange noise reached his ears above the powerful roar of his Bentley rotary engine.

It sounded like someone knocking on a stone with a hammer at incredible speed. He was wondering vaguely what it could be, when, with a loud *whang*! the altimeter, which he happened to be watching, flew to pieces in a little shower of broken glass and metal.

He started so violently that he automatically jerked back in his seat, unconsciously pulling the control-stick back at the same time. The movement undoubtedly saved his life, for, looking over the side of his cockpit, he was just in time to see two lines of glittering sparks streaking across the spot where he had been a fraction of a second before. And then his eye fell on something else—something that brought his heart to his mouth and made him stare in blank astonishment.

He would have been prepared to swear that there was not another machine in the sky except his own, but there, not fifty yards away, was a large green aeroplane

21

with a huge black cross on its side. It was a two-seater, and as he stared in horrified amazement, the gunner in the rear cockpit was calmly removing empty ammunition drums and replacing them with new ones.

Vaguely, at the back of his mind, Henry felt sure that he ought to do something, but for the life of him he could not think what it was. His brain refused to act. Uppermost in his mind was the certain knowledge that within the next three seconds that calm, dispassionate, muffled figure in the back seat would direct a deadly stream of bullets at him. He shifted his gaze to the pilot, and stared fascinated at the distorted eyes of the German glaring at him through the big round goggles above a flowing blond moustache.

Henry waited for no more. Just what stunt he did he could never afterwards say, but he admitted frankly that he pulled, pushed, and stepped on everything within reach. Even as he shot up in a crazy loop came the knowledge that he, too, had a gun, and could shoot back.

Quivering with excitement, he levelled out, gripped the Bowden lever* of his guns, and tore back at the green machine. It was not there. He pushed up his goggles and looked again, unable to believe his eyes. Where the green machine had been there now stretched an infinite expanse of gleaming white mist, and above, the pale-blue wintry sky.

'This isn't flying, it's conjuring!' he groaned. 'Where the dickens can he have got to?'

He leaned far over the side of the cockpit, searching high and low for his attacker. He had just decided, with

* The 'trigger' to fire the machine guns, usually fitted to the pilot's control column.

22

infinite relief, that in some unaccountable manner it had disappeared, when a sharp staccato stutter, louder than before, smote his ears.

He jumped violently and looked again over the other side. The green machine was almost on top of him, bearing straight down on him, a streak of orange flame leaping from the pilot's gun on the engine cowling.

At the sight a feeling of uncontrollable rage swept over Henry

'What do you think you are—a jack-in-the-box?' he snarled furiously, and flung the Camel round in its own length, at the same time grabbing for his gun lever. The chattering throb of his own guns almost startled him.

In his heart he felt quite certain that they were going to collide. It seemed unavoidable. But, remembering Biggles' instructions about not turning away from a head-on attack, he did not swerve an inch. He had a fleeting vision of two wheels missing his top plane by six inches as the other machine swept up over him. He was round in a flash, blind rage swamping all other emotions.

'Go about smashing people's altimeters, would you, you dirty dog?' he muttered, as his eye fell on the German diving steeply towards the clouds.

He thrust his control-stick forward in an endeavour to overtake it, but before he could reach it the other plane had plunged out of sight into the mist, where he knew it would be useless to follow, and he turned away disconsolately.

As he looked around, he realised with something of a shock that he was by no means certain of his position, but he struck off in what he thought was the right direction for the German aerodrome. He kept a wary eye on

23

the sky, and got the fright of his life when three S.E.5's*
burst out of the fog just in front of him. His heart was
still palpitating when the pilots waved a cheery greeting
to him as they passed.

'Well, according to my reckoning, that German aerodrome can't be far away now!' he thought, and, throt-
tling back, he dropped down through the unbroken sea
of cloud. As he came out, he looked below hopefully. It
was nearly dark, but there, sure enough, was a row of
drab hangars on the edge of an aerodrome.

'And Biggles said I couldn't find my way!' he scoffed,
as he put his nose down in a deep dive. 'They haven't
found it themselves yet, anyway!' he muttered, noting
the undisturbed atmosphere on the ground.

To and fro across the sheds he dived, working his
bomb-toggle swiftly until all eight bombs had been
released. He looked below with profound interest as he
climbed once more for the clouds, but found to his
bitter disappointment that the smoke from his bursting
bombs had obscured the view. Dimly, he could just
make out groups of men rushing about like ants, pouring out of hangars and huts and waving their arms at
him furiously.

'Ha, ha!' he smiled. 'Hold that little lot!' And then,
realising it would be unwise to tempt Providence by
staying in the vicinity too long, he soared into the sunlight above the clouds and headed for home.

He was not quite certain of the direction, but he knew
that by flying on a south-westerly course he would at
least reach the British Lines and safety, after which it
would not take him long to find his own aerodrome at

* Scouting experimental single-seater British biplane fighter in service
1917–1920, fitted with two or three machine guns.

Maranique. With his lips pursed in an inaudible whistle and his heart bounding with the joy of a job well done, he dropped once more through the mist in search of home.

Biggles and Algy were also racing home above the mist, with that curious certainty of position which some airmen seem to possess. After gliding through the concealing curtain of cloud, they picked up the aerodrome, landed, and taxied quickly towards the waiting mechanics.

'What a mess we made!' laughed Biggles, as they climbed out of their machines. 'Hallo, the Professor's back—there's his bus.' As he opened the door of the ante-room, he turned to Algy, finger on lips. A voice was speaking. It was Henry's.

'No, sir,' Henry was saying. 'I didn't see them again after we entered the clouds, so I followed my own course. I found the Hun aerodrome and dropped my bombs, but visibility was so bad that I was unable to form a reliable estimate of the damage.'

Biggles pushed the door wide open. Henry and Major Mullen were standing in the middle of the room, surrounded by a circle of pilots.

'So you found it all right?' said Biggles, keeping a straight face with an effort.

'Of course. Worked out mathematically, it was impossible to miss it,' replied Henry casually.

Biggles turned to a window to watch an S.E.5 land on the aerodrome and taxi, tail-up, towards the mess. A moment later, Major Sharp, of Squadron No. 287, breathing heavily, stood swaying on the threshold. He appeared to have some difficulty in finding his voice. Biggles, a grim suspicion already forming in his mind,

25

turned a questioning eye on Henry, and showed his teeth in a mirthless grin.

'Which of you fools has been fanning my aerodrome?' barked the major.

There was a silence which could be felt.

'Eight confounded great holes all over the aerodrome! Fortunately nobody hurt. It'll take my men all day to fill 'em in. It was a Camel—we saw it—no argument! Its number was—er—er—'

'J–7743,' muttered Biggles involuntarily.

'How do you know that?' cried Henry hotly. 'That's the number of my machine!'

'Oh, mathematics—purely a matter of mathematics!' said Biggles softly.

The telephone rang shrilly, and Major Mullen picked up the receiver.

'Hallo!' he said. 'Yes—what's that? Good show—just a minute, and I'll ask them.' He turned towards the other pilots in the room.

'Did you have a go at a green Hannoverana* this afternoon, Biggles? The artillery are on the line, and they report a green Hannoverana crashed on landing about half an hour ago, near Saint Pol. The engine was shot to bits and the gunner was dead.'

'No, I haven't seen a two-seater,' replied Biggles, in astonishment.

'Nor I,' admitted Algy.

'It's all right—I got it,' said Henry casually.

'What! Did you shoot at a green Hannoverana this afternoon?' cried Biggles, in amazement.

'I did,' replied Henry modestly, 'and the last I saw of it, it was going down through the clouds.'

---

* German two-seater fighter and ground attack biplane.

'By the anti-clockwise propeller of my sainted aunt! You must have hit it. How on earth did you manage that?' almost shouted Biggles.

'Oh, mathematics—it was purely a matter of mathematics,' replied Henry, grinning, as a howl of laughter split the air.

'Mathematics, my eye! How did you work it out, anyway?' snorted Biggles.

'Well, it was this way,' replied Henry modestly. 'This Boche thought he was smart. He seemed to think that one Hannoverana plus one Camel only equalled one Hannoverana, which, as Euclid would say, is absurd. I got angry, and decided to show him where he was wrong, and that one Camel plus one Hannoverana equalled one Camel!'

'Yes, I know!' jeered Biggles. 'So you placed the point A upon the point B, so that the line A—B fell along the line—Bah! Never mind about the ABC stuff. Whereabouts along the Lines did *he* fall? That's what I want to know.'

'I don't know, and that's a fact,' admitted Henry, grinning. 'Our position was not included in the data. To tell you the truth, I didn't know where I was—and I didn't much care. The thing that annoyed me was that he popped about so fast that I hadn't time to prove my theorem.'

'I had an idea you'd discover that,' grinned Biggles. 'But how did you get him at the finish?'

'Well, if I must tell the truth,' he grinned, 'I threw my copybook at the cloud and went for him bald-headed. I let drive with my Vickers, and down he went, and that was that. I didn't know I'd hit him. He just buzzed off into the soup, where I couldn't follow him,

27

and that's the last I saw of him. Then I beetled around until I found the aerodrome and unloaded my eggs*—'

'I think the less you say about that the better,' advised Biggles, with a sidelong glance at the major. 'The point is, you got a Hun, and if you'll leave your copybook at home in future, follow me, and do your fighting by the baldheaded method, you can come with me to-morrow. Is it a go?'

'It is!' declared Henry emphatically.

* Slang: bombs.

28

Chapter 2
The Joy-ride

Biggles sat on a chock outside A Flight hangar, and surveyed the jazz camouflage pattern on the wilting canvas of the temporary structure disconsolately.

'The fact is,' he said moodily to the little group of pilots who were lounging about the tarmac between patrols, 'this war isn't what it used to be. There seems to be a sort of blight settling over it. Why, I remember the day when you couldn't stick your nose over the Line without butting into a bit of fun of some sort or another. Now you trail up and down, and if you do see a Hun he's gone before you can pass the time of day.

'I don't know what's come over 'em—not that we do anything very clever, if it comes to that. Escort*— escort—escort—always blinking well escort. I'm sick of beetling along behind a lot of Nines. There was a time when you could go where you liked and do what you liked and no one to say how, where, or why, so long as you got a Hun once in a while.

'Now, what with half the old crowd gone west** or gone home, and thousands of spare brass-hats*** looking for jobs, it's escort every blinking day. That's about as far as their imagination goes. It makes me tired. I hear old Wilks, of Squadron No. 287, actually got

* Single-seat fighter that flew with observer or bombing aircraft to protect against enemy attack.
** Slang: dead.
*** Slang: a staff officer (who wore gold braid on his service cap).

29

strafed the other day for shooting up a Jerry aerodrome alone. Said he ought to wait for orders or something. By the way, where have they put that Albatros you brought down yesterday, Algy?' he asked suddenly.

'Along in old C Flight hangar,' replied Algy.

'Let's go and have a look at it,' suggested Biggles, rising.

The group wended is way towards the last hangar in the line where the captured red-nosed Albatros plane poked round a fold in the canvas.

'Where did you hit him, Algy?' asked Biggles, as he examined the machine with interest.

'I didn't. His engine stopped running on the top of a stall, and just glided down comfortable-like,' responded Algy, with a broad grin.

'Really! Then the machine's O.K.?'

'Should be.'

'Come on, let's start her up, for a joke!' cried Biggles, with a flash of inspiration.

'I shouldn't, if I were you,' broke in Mahoney. 'Wing'll* probably be fetching her this afternoon.'

'Wing be dashed! Whose aeroplane is it, anyway?' growled Biggles, as he clambered into the wooden fuselage and juggled about with the controls. 'Give me a swing, Algy**!' he called.

The engine started with a roar, and Biggles grinned delightedly as the group behind him staggered out of the slipstream. Suddenly the grin grew broader, and he glanced at the wind stocking. It hung motionless.

---

* The administrative headquarters—each 'wing' commanded several squadrons.
** The engines of all the fighter or scout aircraft of the First World War were started by rapidly turning the propeller by hand.

'Look out—I'm off!' he yelled, and pulled the throttle open.

The German Albatros sped across the aerodrome like a bullet, and soared into the air. Something spanged through the fuselage behind him, and the pilot looked down with a start. A squad of British troops, evidently returning from the Line, were passing up the narrow road which skirted the aerodrome, and the stabbing flashes of rifle-fire warned him of his danger. He was in an enemy plane—and naturally the troops were firing at it!

'My hat!' he muttered as he pulled the control-stick back and zoomed swiftly. 'Let's get out of this!'

A cloud of white smoke* blossomed out in front of him, another, and another, each one closer than the last, and he dodged wildly into the clouds which half-covered the sky, to avoid the bursts of anti-aircraft gun-fire.

'Best shooting I've ever seen 'em make!' he muttered grimly. 'They'll probably hit me in a minute. I must have been crazy to take this kite off the floor. How am I going to get back? That's the question!'

He climbed slowly in ever-widening circles as he pondered the question, anxiously scanning the sky in every direction. He started as his eye fell on a speck in the distance. It was an R.E.8** describing figures of eight as it ploughed a lonely course on a shoot*** for the

---

* In general, British anti-aircraft fire gave off white smoke and German anti-aircraft fire gave off black smoke.

** British two-seater biplane designed for reconnaissance and artillery observations.

*** An aircraft pinpointing a target for the artillery below. The pilot would check how close the shells were falling to the target, then signal to the gunners below using morse code transmitted by radio.

31

artillery. He was about to turn away when something else caught his eye—a cluster of specks moving fast into the sun, in line with the R.E.8.

'Huns!' he ejaculated. 'And that fool observer hasn't spotted them. He must be asleep!' Automatically he raced in the direction of the lone British machine.

In his excitement, the fact that he was flying a black-crossed machine—marking it as German, of course—completely slipped from his mind, but a flashing streak of tracer bullets across his nose, delivered by the gunner in the rear cockpit of the R.E.8, reminded him, and he dodged away quickly. The R.E.8 pilot waited for no more, but dived for home, the observer grinding out the remainder of the drum of ammunition at long range as he went. Biggles watched its departure with a smile, satisfied that his arrival had served its purpose.

'He's out of harm's way now, anyway,' he muttered. 'Hallo—'

He blinked in startled surprise as a green Albatros swam into view a bare hundred feet away. The pilot was gesticulating wildly. Biggles instinctively groped for his triggers, but, suddenly remembering the circum-stances, released them wonderingly.

'I can't get the hang of this!' he groaned. He glanced to the right, and started again in dismay. German Alba-troses were all round him. 'So I'm flying in a blinking Hun formation, eh?' he gasped, trying to grasp the situ-ation. 'This is getting me all groggy. What's he waving about, I wonder?' he muttered, staring at the leader of the enemy formation. 'Peeved because I scared his bird, I suppose. I'd better see about getting out of this—but it won't do to be in too much of a hurry.'

32

The Boche* machines had once more settled down to steady flight, and he kept his position, glancing furtively from left to right at the strange faces around him. It took him a full five minutes to become accustomed to the position, then a slow grin spread over his face.

'And I've just been saying that things aren't what they used to be! Why, there never were such times!' he thought. A movement on the part of the leader caused him to look down. Another R.E.8 was cruising to and fro as it signalled to the gunners.

'How any of these kites are left in the sky beats me. They must fly with their eyes shut!' muttered Biggles, as he tore down and sent a warning stream of tracer bullets across the nose of the unsuspecting machine. Pulling up steeply, he narrowly escaped collision with the rest of the enemy formation. The R.E. pilot streaked for home as if he had had a glimpse of the devil. Again the leader swung close to Biggles, making violent signals.

'If I do that again he'll be shooting me down, and I don't wonder,' Biggles reflected, sympathising with the man's just cause for anger. He realised that it must have been annoying in the extreme for the other man to have some fool in the formation who made a premature attack and scared the other machine away before an effective attack could be launched.

He realised, also, that he was in a very awkward position. Even if he was able to reach the British Lines safely, it would lead to all sorts of complications if the Germans ever discovered that a British officer had been flying a German machine.

Quite apart from the fact that it would bring disgrace

* Slang: derogatory term for Germans.

33

on the whole British Service for an officer, other than a Secret Service agent, to fly an enemy machine over hostile country, he would certainly get in hot water himself if the authorities discovered the culprit—as they undoubtedly would. Once such a practice was started there was no telling where it would stop; an impossible state of affairs might easily be created. No man would trust another in the air, irrespective of the type of machine or nationality marks, and it might end by friends shooting each other down by accident on mere suspicion. People would shoot first and ask questions afterwards.

No. It was a bad business, from which he must extricate himself with the least possible delay. How to do it was the question. Obviously he could not just fly back behind the British Lines and land under the very noses of the Germans, who could not fail to see him from the air. They would remember the colour of the machine, possibly the number on it, and inquiries would speedily reveal that it had not returned from its last patrol, and a shrewd suspicion as to the true state of affairs would inevitably result.

Even now there was the possibility of one of the German pilots with whom he was flying recognising the machine as one which had been reported missing. In fact, one of them, in a bright yellow machine, had twice come very close indeed, with his goggles raised as if he was trying to ascertain the identity of the pilot.

Biggles turned his collar a little higher, and got well down into the cockpit. 'I am a poor prune,' he muttered, 'getting myself into this mess. I shall have to get out of it, that's all.'

Rather than incur suspicion by turning away now, he

decided to stay with them until well over the German Lines, and then turn away, as if he was going to another German aerodrome. The thing that worried him most was whether the machine he was flying had belonged to the circus* he was with; if so, the very act of leaving them would in itself be suspicious.

He breathed a sigh of relief when the leader swung round and headed towards the German support trenches, and he began to drop back at once, with a view to quietly fading away the moment a reasonable opportunity presented itself. It was with no small apprehension that he noticed the pilot in the yellow machine was dropping back also, and, although it might be pure chance, he seemed to be taking care to keep between Biggles and the British Lines—a position which would effectually prevent the British pilot from creeping away unobserved.

A few minutes passed, and Biggles could stand the suspense no longer. He decided at all costs to find out whether the Boche in the yellow machine was really suspicious, or whether it was his own guilty imagination. He was not kept long in doubt, for the moment he turned the yellow machine turned with him, and this move threw Biggles into a worse position than ever.

He could not bring himself to commit the unpardonable offence of shooting down a German from a German machine. Yet what was he to do if the Boche suddenly turned on him? One thing was certain. If the Boche got back home, then the cat would be out of the bag with a vengeance. More than ever, he regretted the foolish impulse which had resulted in his present absurd predicament.

* Slang: a formation of German fighter aircraft.

He looked across at the other pilot, who was now flying not more than twenty feet away, and he could almost imagine what the other was thinking. He was suspicious, that was obvious; he might even have been a personal friend of the man who had previously flown the machine which the British pilot was now flying. Yet he could not bring himself to shoot at the machine on suspicion alone.

Biggles guessed he was waiting to ascertain if the machine *was* going back, and he knew instinctively that the moment he reached the Lines and made the first move to cross over the German would shoot. He wondered vaguely what the troops in the trenches would think when they saw the unbelievable spectacle of two Albatroses fighting each other.

It is perhaps curious that the one event which could solve the problem never occurred to him, and he could never afterwards understand why such an obvious possibility did not strike him. As a matter of fact, the next move in the amazing cycle of events came with such a shock that for the moment he simply did not know how to act.

The first indication he had of it was the vicious stutter of guns close at hand, and he caught his breath as a British S.E.5 tore past, a bare thirty feet away. Both he and the pilot of the yellow German machine had been so interested in each other that they had been caught napping. Biggles glanced upwards. Five or six more S.E.s were dropping like vultures out of the sky.

Rat-tat-tat-tat! Rat-tat-tat-tat! Biggles groaned as the first S.E. swung round at him, guns streaming tracer bullets. 'It must be Wilks and his crowd,' he thought bitterly. Now thoroughly alarmed, he skidded

36

wildly away from the dog-fight and raced nose down for the Line. But escape was not to be so simple. A sharp staccato rattle of guns and a flack-flack-flack-flack behind him sent him half-rolling frantically away from a blue-nosed S.E that was spitting a stream of death and destruction at him.

'Wilks himself!' gasped Biggles. 'Wilks!' he roared desperately, but quite aware of the futility of his appeal. He looked down quickly and saw they were immediately over No Man's Land*. Nearly panicking, for the first time in his life, he threw the machine into a spin, came out, spun again, pulled out again, then zigzagged for the Line.

He had a fleeting vision of the yellow German machine roaring down in a sheet of flame, but he had no time to dwell on it. It looked as if he was likely to follow it to a similar fate. The other British S.E.s were hemming him in, and their nearness at least helped to keep the anti-aircraft gunners from getting busy.

The last thousand feet were a nightmare for Biggles. He stunted as he had never stunted before, and the fact that he was unaccustomed to the controls of the German machine he was flying made the exhibition still more alarming.

Falling out of a wild loop, he looked around anxiously. The S.E. was still on his tail, coming in again to deliver the final blow. In the almost hopeless anxiety of the moment Biggles got an inspiration. Thrusting himself as far up in the cockpit as he could he raised both arms above his head as a signal of surrender. As he hoped, Wilks sheered off, pointing downwards.

Biggles needed no second invitation. A useful-looking

---

* The area of ground between the opposing armies.

37

field swept into view below, and he side-slipped steeply towards it; but as he flattened out he realised that he had come in much too fast. The hedge seemed to rush towards him. There was a crash of breaking wood and rending fabric as he plunged nose first into it.

For a moment he sat quite still, dazed, hardly daring to believe in his good fortune at being still alive. He could no longer hear the S.E.'s engine.

'Gone home to tell the boys about it, I expect,' he muttered, as he painfully removed a long bramble from his face. A voice near at hand made him jump nervously.

'Hi, Jerry! Come out of that!' it yelled.

Before he had time to move, a hand clutched his hair and jerked him bodily from the cockpit. He let out a yell of agony and, turning, looked into the red and panting face of the S.E. flight commander.

Wilks stopped panting. He stopped breathing. A look of incredulous amazement crept over his face. He opened his mouth to speak, but no words came.

'Who do you think you're knocking about?' snarled Biggles. 'Can't a fellow have a joy-ride without your crowd butting in and spoiling it?'

Chapter 3
The Bridge Party

The evening patrol had just come home; Biggles paused in the act of kicking the ante-room fire into a blaze.

'There are,' he announced to the semicircle of officers seated around the fire, 'two sorts of pilots.'

'Now, who told you that?' asked Mahoney in mock astonishment.

'There are the mugs—and the other sort,' concluded Biggles, ignoring the interruption and giving the fire a final kick.

'What's the difference, Biggles?' asked Algy Montgomery, curiously.

'Very little, son, very little,' replied Biggles, with fatherly condescension. 'The mugs go west a little before the others, that's all.'

'What class do I come in?' asked Algy, grinning.

'Oh, you're one of the mugs,' answered Biggles, without the slightest hesitation.

'Then why am I still here?' inquired Algy, glancing around like a barrister addressing a jury.

'The Professor'—Biggles' eyes twinkled as they roved around the circle and came to rest on Henry Watkins—'the Professor will tell you that there is an exception to every rule,' he observed. 'You're it!'

'And what about me?' asked Henry, a trifle anxiously.

'You!' Biggles grinned. 'You're as mad as a hatter. Just listen to this, chaps. Listen while I tell you of

39

something I saw to-day. I saw a Camel plane shooting up the bridge on the Lille road. Was this Camel shooting up the bridge in the orthodox manner, like I should, or you, Mac, or you, Mahoney, or any other sane person, which is by flying up and down it? No, sir, he was flying to and fro across it.

'Great Scott! How many Huns did you reckon to hit that way, Henry? Or were you just counting 'em before you started, so that you could do it by mathematics?' he concluded.

'Never you mind,' replied Henry, flushing. 'You haven't done a lot to it yourself, anyway. I know for a fact you've had three goes at that bridge, ever since Wing said they wanted it blown up!'

A howl of laughter followed this sally, and it was Biggles' turn to flush.

'You're right, kid,' he acknowledged, 'but if you look closely you'll see that I've put a bit of backward stagger on the guard-house at the end!'

'That isn't the bridge,' protested Henry.

'Well, it's more than you've done, anyway,' parried Biggles.

'Maybe it is, but I haven't finished yet,' said Henry, darkly.

'Ha! Did you hear that? He hasn't finished. I'll bet he's going to take a slide-rule over to measure it first,' grinned Biggles. 'Is that what you were doing this morning?'

'Possibly, possibly,' admitted Henry, with a solemn face in spite of the broad grins around him. 'But I'll tell you this, Biggles. If you want to get that bridge you'll have to be mighty quick. She won't be there to-morrow!'

'You mean you won't be *here*!' jeered Biggles.

'Well, let's wait and see,' said Henry, rising. 'I'm off to bed.'

Biggles paused in the work of supervising the adjustment of the Cooper bombs on the racks under his lower planes, and as he did so his eye fell on Henry and a mechanic struggling with a large torpedo-shaped object under the fuselage of Henry's Camel. He took a pace nearer and confirmed his suspicions. The object was a 50-lb high explosive bomb.

'What do you think you're going to do with that thing?' he asked anxiously.

Henry wiped a smear of perspiration from his face with a gauntlet and left a streak of oil in its place. 'I'm going to plant this little squib where it should provide the gentlemen over the way with a pyrotechnic display of unprecedented dimensions,' he announced solemnly, resuming his task.

'When you've finished playing darts with those boy-sized missiles of yours, Biggles, you can stand back and watch my fireworks!'

'You be careful what you're doing with that thing,' Biggles cautioned him soberly. 'If we run into a bunch of Huns, don't you come barging about near me if you've still got that thing on your undercart. And keep your hand off the bomb-toggle until I'm well up out of the way!' he snapped.

Five minutes later, the morning patrol, consisting of Biggles, Algy and Henry, was in the air, climbing quickly for height as it headed towards the enemy Lines—and the bridge which headquarters had marked for destruction. Except for some severe archie as they crossed the Line, they reached it without incident, and signs of the bridge were at once visible.

41

For an area of a mile around the structure the earth was pitted with holes of various sizes made by the British air bombs. As they approached, it was evident that the recent aerial activity above the bridge had not been lost on the enemy and that steps had been taken to give future visitors a warm reception.

Even Biggles hesitated for a moment before the storm of archie and 'flaming onions*' that tore the sky around them.

'Well, I'm not taking this load of bombs back home,' he told himself harshly, and, thrusting the control-stick forward, he tore down at the bridge.

Something jarred the Camel from end to end and he snatched a fleeting glance at his upper port wing, where a strip of trailing fabric told its own story. At four hundred feet he flattened out, took the bridge at the junction of his lower wing and the fuselage, and pulled the bomb-toggle, one—two—three—four. He jerked the control-stick back into his stomach in an almost vertical zoom, and, glancing down, snorted his disgust.

Three swirling rings of foam churned the water and showed where his bombs had fallen into the river which flowed beneath the bridge. The fourth had exploded harmlessly on the bank some distance beyond it.

Again he roared down and, hurtling through the vicious machine-gun barrage near the ground, delivered his last four bombs at point-blank range. Again he glanced over his shoulder as he twisted upwards, and a snarl of disappointment broke from his lips.

The bridge was still standing, apparently intact,

---

* Slang: a type of incendiary anti-aircraft shell only used by the Germans.

while a line of still-smoking holes on the bank showed where his bombs had again missed their mark.

Algy was now busy, and Biggles watched him anxiously as he dodged through the swirling archie smoke. Again he snorted impatiently as he saw Algy's Cooper bombs bursting close to the bridge, but not one of them touched the bridge itself. Where was Henry?

Even as the thought struck him he saw the Professor going down in a vertical dive.

'The crazy fool,' grated Biggles through his teeth, 'he'll go right into the floor at that rate, with that load on!'

A stabbing flame and the vicious crack of a close burst of archie made him swerve wildly for a moment, and he eyed another gash in his wing fabric anxiously. It was near the leading edge, and he knew there was always a danger of the whole wing fabric 'ballooning' if the air rushed into it.

'This is a fool's game. I'm getting out of it!' he muttered, and a swift glance revealed Algy above him, streaking out of the danger zone. He hastened after him, then looked down for Henry's Camel, and an exclamation of amazement broke from his lips. He thrust up his goggles with a quick movement to see better, and he stared hard, almost unable to believe the evidence of his own eyes.

The centre of the bridge had completely disappeared, and a large cloud of smoke was drifting away from the ruins. But of Henry's Camel there was no sign!

As Biggles sped out of the sea of archie bursts, he looked around with ever-increasing anxiety, but there was no sign of the missing Camel. Algy was still circling for height—the only other machine in the sky beside his

43

own. His practised eye searched the ground, field by field, tree by tree, for a mile or more around the bridge, but there was no sign of a crash.

Puzzled, he turned homewards, knowing there was just a chance that Henry had hopped across the hedges out of view, while he himself was busily engaged in dodging archie.

He landed, and sat on the 'hump' of his Camel behind the cockpit, until Algy had landed and taxied quickly alongside. Slowly he unfastened and removed his cap and goggles.

'What happened to him?' he asked quietly.

'I dunno!' replied Algy laconically. 'The last I saw of him, he was going down like a sack of bricks. I turned away out of the archie, and when I looked back again he wasn't there—neither was the bridge, for that matter,' he concluded, tapping a cigarette on the back of his hand.

'What on earth can have happened to him?' muttered Biggles, with a worried frown. 'He's down somewhere, or he would be home by now, that's certain. We'd better go back and have another look round.'

They hurried back to the bridge, and for more than an hour they flew up and down, in spite of the archie, searching the whole area systematically for signs of the crashed Camel, but without success.

Once, while Biggles was examining a wood closely, the archies died away suddenly, and he acted with the lightning-like speed born of long experience, without looking around to discover the reason. He flung the control-stick right over to the left, and then back into his right side, kicking out his right foot at the same time.

The Camel swung up in a swift barrel-roll. He was

44

just in time. There was a shrill chatter of guns from somewhere near at hand, and a red-nosed Pfalz* scout roared past in a wire-screaming dive.

'Nearly caught me napping, did you?' thought Biggles grimly, as he flung the Camel on the tail of the now zooming Hun. 'Looking for trouble, eh? Well, you can have it! What's Algy doing? He ought to have attended to you.'

He lifted his arm in front of his face and squinted through the outstretched fingers of his gauntleted hand into the sun. He grinned as he saw a Camel standing on its nose, roaring down at the German plane.

But the Boche pilot had seen it too, and, regretting his indiscretion, was diving in a panic for the ground. Biggles and Algy both had height and speed of him, and were on his tail in an instant. The Boche hadn't a chance. Glancing over his shoulder, he looked death in the face, in the shape of two pairs of Vickers guns not a hundred feet behind him.

As he looked back, Biggles and Algy simultaneously started pumping lead through their props**. The Boche slumped forward in his seat. The dive of the Pfalz plane became steeper and steeper, until it was plunging down to oblivion at frightful speed in a vertical dive.

Biggles saw the top plane swing back as the black-crossed enemy machine broke up in the air, and then he pulled up in a steep, climbing turn, beckoning to Algy to follow him. A tornado of archie broke loose from the

---

* German single-seater biplane fighter with two or three machine guns synchronised to fire through the propeller.
** Slang: firing through their propellers.

45

infuriated gunners on the ground who had witnessed the tragic end of the Boche machine.

'Pah!' snorted Biggles disgustedly, as he twisted and turned to throw the gunners off their mark. 'That was too much like murder for my liking. The Huns must be putting babies into some of their kites!'

An archie exploded not twenty feet below him, and the force of the explosion nearly turned him over. In a sudden fit of passion, he tore down at the stab of flame that revealed the position of the gun on the ground.

'Let's see how you like it!' he gritted, as he thumbed the gun lever. 'How do you like that, eh?' he went on, as a double streak of tracer bullets ripped and tore the earth about the gun, which he now saw was of the mobile type, mounted on a lorry.

That the gunners did not like it was at once evident, for the driver of the lorry set off down the road at full speed.

'You can't get away like that!' muttered Biggles coldly, and held his dive until he was a bare fifty feet behind the hurrying vehicle.

The German gunners could hardly be blamed for losing their nerve. The lorry swerved dangerously — once — twice — and then, crashing into the ditch that ran beside the road, it overturned and flung the driver and crew into the hedge.

The sight of a column of German infantry brought Biggles to his senses

'I must be crazy, coming right down so far over the Line!' he muttered, looking around to see if Algy had followed him. He discovered the other Camel still at his wing-tip. The pilot was making frantic signals and pointing.

Biggles, following the outstretched finger, saw a line

of swiftly approaching black specks above them, and their straight wings told him all he wanted to know. They were Fokkers*! He whirled the Camel round in its own length, and raced back to the Lines, emptying his guns into the Boche trenches as he roared across them to safety.

Algy looked at him coldly after they had landed and taxied in.

'What's gone wrong with you, Biggles?' he asked. 'I wish you'd warn me when you're going to do things like that. I'll get myself a pair of tin pants made if I've got to fly with you much longer,' he went on, as he climbed stiffly from his seat.

'Are you hurt?' asked Biggles quickly.

'No, only a scratch, but it happens to be where I sit down,' replied Algy. 'But what else can you expect if you will go footling about fifty feet above the whole blinkin' German Army?'

'Did you see any signs of a Camel on the ground?' asked Biggles.

'No,' Algy said. 'I can't make it out—and that's a fact!'

Inquiries soon revealed that Henry had not returned, and Biggles buried his chin between his palms sadly as he squatted down on a chock. 'The Professor's gone, I'm afraid,' he said. 'But I'm dashed if I can understand what happened!'

Refusing to give up hope, they lounged about the tarmac silently, their hearts sinking with the sun, but hoping against hope that the missing bird would come home to roost.

---

* German fighter with three wings with two forward-firing guns. Their slang name was tripehounds. See front cover for illustration.

47

'Come on, laddie, it's no use waiting any longer,' said Biggles at last, as twilight deepened into night. And together they made their way slowly to the mess.

'Well, it beats me!' said Biggles, several hours later, as he kicked the ante-room fire into a blaze with the heel of his shoe. The scene was the same as it had been the previous night at the same hour, except that Henry's face was missing. 'I can't make it out. If I was not sure that Henry wasn't the sort to commit suicide, I should say that he deliberately charged the bridge and knocked the whole works into the river.

'He was diving as if that was what he intended to do. But why take a bomb? What happened to the machine? There isn't a sign of it anywhere, as anybody can see for himself. I'll bet you that he had one of his fool schemes worked out on paper and it came unstuck. That was it.'

'You're right, Biggles, that was it,' said a sombre voice from the doorway.

Biggles stood as if turned to stone, his foot poised over the fire. The others stared at a mud-stained, blood-stained, dishevelled figure in the doorway with expressions of mingled alarm and amazement.

Henry! There was a crash of falling chairs in the wild stampede that followed. In a moment everybody was laughing and talking together to the comrade whom they had given up for lost.

'Mind my head, chaps, it's sore! Give me a hot drink,' said Henry wearily. 'I want a bath and some grub, and then I'll tell you how it came unstuck.'

'I worked it out this way,' began Henry an hour later. The mud had been removed and a bandage decorated his forehead. 'I noticed that everybody went for that bridge from up top-sides.'

'Well, how else—' broke in Biggles.

'Wait a minute,' continued Henry impatiently. 'The Huns had therefore concentrated all their dirty work— archie, machine-guns, and so on—to face the danger from that direction. Now it seemed to me that if an attack was made from underneath, it would not only upset their calculations, but a well-placed bomb would do more damage in the foundations than it would from up top. So I took a fifty-pounder with a fifteen seconds' delay fuse.'

'But underneath!' cried Biggles. 'How do you mean, underneath?'

'Well, instead of flying over it like everybody else did, I decided to fly up the river and underneath it. That's all.' He paused to relight his cigarette.

'Good heavens! I always knew you were off your rocker!' declared Biggles, with conviction.

'All went well, according to plan, until I reached the bridge,' continued Henry. 'And that's where I came unstuck—in every sense of the word,' he said sadly. 'The arch wasn't wide enough for me to get through!'

A yell of laughter split the air.

'It's all very well for you to laugh,' cried Henry hotly, 'but it was no joke, I can tell you!'

'I'll bet it wasn't!' agreed Biggles warmly. 'What did you do?'

'Do! Do! Dash it! What could I do? I didn't discover it until too late. It was either hit a buttress or the hole. I chose the hole,' he said simply.

'So should I, every time,' agreed Biggles.

'Don't ask me what happened,' Henry went on. 'I'd already got hold of the bomb-toggle and I suppose I

49

must have pulled it. The next thing I knew there was one dickens of a crash, and my wings had gone. The fuselage, with me in it, didn't stop. We went right on. Boy, you should have seen me take the water. A torpedo wasn't in it. Talk about "Twenty thousand leagues under the sea"!'

'Joined the submarine service, eh?' grinned Biggles.

'I did,' acknowledged Henry. 'Fortunately, the river was in spate, and the next thing I knew I was floating down the river hanging on to a wheel trying to look like a bit of wreckage. And I didn't have to try very hard. I drifted into the rushes, and lay there, with just my nose sticking out, like a blinking alligator, wondering what had happened.

'A crowd of Huns were laughing like fun on the bank, as well they might, but luckily at that moment a formation of Nines* rolled up. That stopped 'em laughing. It stopped me laughing, too, if it comes to that. Those Nines unloaded about ten tons of perdition on the bridge, and I expect they'll claim they got it.'

'They won't!' said Biggles grimly. 'I'll see to that!'

'Well,' continued Henry, 'in the hullabaloo, I hoofed it down the river to a wood, where I got out of my Sidcot** and started off towards the balloon line, which I could see. I started crawling along ditches, and I crawled for miles. I crawled till I couldn't crawl any longer, and then I got up and walked.

'I thought I'd be spotted at once, but I couldn't crawl any longer; I'm no snake. First I passed a couple of Hun officers. I saluted, but they didn't even look at me.

---

* De Havilland 9's—two-seater British bomber with one fixed forward-firing gun for the pilot, plus a rear mobile gun for the observer.
** A thick padded garment worn by airmen.

50

I passed a lot of troops, and a sergeant-major looked at me a bit old-fashioned—because I looked such a shocking mess, I expect. After all, they wouldn't expect me to be strolling about their reserve lines, would they?'

'No, you're right, they wouldn't!' muttered Biggles.

'I walked until it was dark, by which time I was pretty near the Front Line, I expect, and then an inferno broke loose. Every gun in France was turned on me—or it seemed like it.

'Naturally, that stirred things up a bit, and it gave me a chance to get moving. I doubled for about a couple of hundred yards, lay doggo while some Boches went past—going the other way for all they were worth—and then carried on.

'I don't know if any of you chaps have ever tried doing a quarter-mile steeplechase through a Crystal Palace firework display. Anyhow, I shifted like the dickens until I came to a trench, then I rested a moment before going on. There didn't seem to be anyone about. I suppose I was lucky.'

'Lucky—I'll say you were!' grunted Algy.

'Well, after that, things started getting a bit warm. There was an appalling bombardment, rifle-fire, a Lewis gun or two, and enough Very* lights to floodlight Hyde Park. I kept it up for about twenty yards, then I came to some wire, which I couldn't get round. So, reckoning I'd had about enough, I found a nice comfortable shell-hole and went to earth. The ground up above wasn't any too healthy just then!

'I've never heard anything like the row. Thank goodness I'm not in the infantry! The next thing I heard was someone shouting in English, and I looked up to see a

* A coloured flare fired as a signal from a special short-barrelled pistol.

51

sergeant. I said,"Hold hard!" and he said: "What the dickens—" And I told him.

'He took me to an officer, a bloke named Davis—nice chap—and then I walked back to the old Front Line. I got a lift on a lorry back here. That's all!'

Chapter 4
The Bottle Party

Algy burst into the officers' mess of No. 266 Squadron like a whirlwind.

'I say, Biggles!' he cried excitedly. 'Have you seen Duneville?'

'No. What's it doing? Running about in circles, taking running snatches at itself?' replied Biggles, looking up from a well-thumbed paper.

'I mean those balloons*,' went on Algy breathlessly.

'Calm yourself, son! What balloons?' asked Biggles, in surprise.

'Three—three blinking sausages all in a row,' declared Algy, 'and one of them has got two baskets on it,' he added vindictively.

'Yes; but what's this got to do with me?' replied Biggles coldly.

Algy stared at him, nonplussed.

'Well—er,' he stammered, 'I—er—thought that particular sausage was your special meat—yours and Wilkinson's of 287.'

'Is that why you didn't have a crack at 'em?' inquired Biggles sarcastically.

'Yes, that and—er—'

---

* Both sides in the First World War used kite or observation balloons, with observers in baskets suspended below the balloon, for spotting artillery and enemy troop movements. Their slang name was sausages.

53

'Go ahead, laddie!' broke in Biggles impatiently. 'Don't stall. What was the other thing?'

'Ten Fokker triplanes cruising above 'em,' admitted Algy reluctantly, with a sheepish smile.

'Bah! You wouldn't let a little thing like that stop you, would you?' said Biggles reprovingly, raising his eyebrows.

'You go and have a smack at 'em yourself—they're still there,' invited Algy. 'If you think—'

A car pulled up outside, and Colonel Raymond, of Wing Headquarters, alighted. He nodded cheerfully to the officers present. 'Where's the major, Bigglesworth?' he asked quickly.

'Isn't he on the tarmac, sir?' asked Biggles.

'Can't see him,' replied the colonel. 'But what I really came over for was to ask if you'd seen—er—'

'The scenery around Duneville?' asked Biggles innocently.

'Then you have?' said the colonel.

Biggles shook his head vigorously.

'No, I haven't,' he denied, 'and, what is more, I don't want to. I don't see the sense in burning good petrol to go all that way just to look at it.'

'Oh, well, I shall have to go on to Squadron No. 287,' observed the colonel sadly; 'they are more accommodating.'

'Wait a minute, sir!' cried Biggles, as the colonel reached the door. 'What's the prize this time for knocking a sausage down?'

'Three days' Paris leave and free transport,' said the colonel promptly.

'Tell Wilks he can have it!' grinned Biggles. 'He knows more about what to do in Paris than I do.

'I'm not getting my eardrums blown out for any three

54

days in Paris,' he declared as the door closed behind the colonel. 'No one but a madman would take on that job. Apart from the Huns upstairs, I bet the ground around the winches of those balloons is so thick with guns that you couldn't walk a yard without stepping on one.

'If anyone tried to get near them, the air would be so stiff with archies and flaming onions that he'd have to fly by compass to get through 'em. No! Not for me!'

'If the Fokkers weren't there and the gunners weren't there, it wouldn't be so hard, would it?' inquired Henry Watkins, known as the Professor, nervously.

'I thought you'd get a rush of blood to the brain!' sneered Biggles. 'What do you suggest doing? Going over and asking them to go away for a bit? Well, go ahead, son—I'm not stopping you.'

'There must be a way,' insisted Henry.

'Well, get out your copy-book and work it out,' invited Biggles.

'Wait—I've got an idea!' cried Henry suddenly.

'I'll bet you have,' jeered Biggles.

'Listen, Biggles! Have you ever blown into an empty bottle?' asked Henry, leaning forward in his chair.

'Blown into an empty bottle! What on earth would I blow into an empty bottle for?' gasped Biggles in amazement.

'I mean when you were at school—blown across the top of one with the cork out?' went on Henry enthusiastically.

'Ah! You mean to make sure there was nothing left in it?' said Biggles, with a flash of inspiration.

'No, you ass—to make it whistle,' Henry retorted.

'But what the dickens would I want to make an empty bottle whistle for?' exclaimed Biggles, in astonishment. 'Oh! You mean to whistle for another full one?'

'No, you idiot!' yelled Henry. 'Just to make a noise.'

'You're barmy—I always knew you were,' declared Biggles. 'What's all this got to do with balloons, anyway?'

'Listen, you poor fish!' said Henry tersely. 'When I was at Thetford, learning to fly—'

'Learning to fly! Did you learn to fly?' gasped Biggles, in mock amazement.

'I wish you wouldn't interrupt!' snarled Henry. 'When I was at Thetford, a fool came over from Narborough, on Christmas morning, and dropped an empty bottle from about ten thousand feet.

'We didn't know it was a bottle. We thought it was just the sky falling down. At first it whistled, then it shrieked, and then it—'

Henry threw up his hands in a despairing gesture.

'The din was like nothing on earth. It made more noise than a score of 230-pound bombs. Now, my point is this: If one bottle can do that, think of the noise two or three dozen bottles would make falling at once!

'I'll bet the gunners would stick their heads in their dugouts when that lot started warbling. They'd go to earth like a lot of rabbits with a terrier around.'

'I get you!' cried Biggles. 'Go on, kid!'

'How many machines can we raise?' asked Henry.

'Nine,' Biggles replied.

'Eight,' corrected MacLaren. 'Mine's having a new tyre put on.'

'Not on your life!' cried Biggles hotly. 'You're not getting away with that, Mac. You take off on bare rims if you can't get off any other way. Nine! Go on, Henry.'

56

'Well, we all go over at the maximum height, and six come up behind the Fokkers,' Henry explained. 'We'll cross over, say, at Hamel, so that they won't see us. Now, let us suppose that each of the six machines has nine bottles. Let me see! That's fifty-four bottles. We'll tie a bit of string round the necks, but keep them separate, so that we can pick up the whole lot in a bunch and drop them overboard together. Now, this is the plan.

'We've all crossed over at Hamel and are approaching the balloons from the German side. The first six machines go on ahead, drop the load of bottles overboard as they pass the balloons, and then dive for home underneath the Fokkers.

'They'll come down, of course, but we can beat them in a dive. They'll break up if they try to catch us. The Fokkers will chase the six machines, and that will take the Fokkers away from the balloons and dispose of one difficulty.

'When the bottles start singing their song of songs, every gunner on the ground for miles will think the sky is falling down on him, and they'll dive into the nearest hole.

'That will leave the way all clear for the other three machines which are in the offing. They make for the sausages—one sausage apiece—and they ought to get them before the Huns see what's up.

'They won't hear the machines coming for the noise of the bottles. How's that?' he concluded triumphantly.

Biggles looked at the speaker approvingly.

'Come on, chaps!' he cried, springing to his feet and starting towards the door. 'Let's go and fill up with Buckingham.'

By 'Buckingham,' Biggles meant a type of incendiary

bullet used only for balloon strafing. Its use was forbidden for any other purpose, and an officer with Buckingham in his machine-gun belts had to carry written orders from his C.O.* that he was balloon strafing—to save him from punishment, perhaps death, if he was captured with the illegal missiles on board.

'Wait a minute! Who's going to do what?' cried Mahoney. 'Let's get this clear at the start.'

'Algy, the Professor, and I will do the shooting, and the rest can carry the bottles,' replied Biggles. 'Algy ought to be able to hit a balloon, if he can't hit anything else. Come on, let's get the bottles.'

The shell-torn village of Hamel lay below. Nine Camels, in a 'layer' formation of six and three, the three underneath, roared across the Lines and headed steadily out into enemy sky. A few minutes later they started to swing round in a wide curve which would bring them up behind Duneville and the balloons.

Biggles, leading, peered ahead through the swirling flash of his propeller, and gave a little grunt of satisfaction as his eyes fell on a large formation of enemy triplanes in the distance.

He glanced over his shoulder, rocked his wings, and altered his course a trifle to place himself directly between the sun and the enemy machines.

His eagle eyes probed the atmosphere under the Fokkers. Ah! There were the balloons, looking from that height like three huge, overgrown mushrooms on the ground.

His eyes returned to the Fokkers, and did not leave them again until the distance between them was little

* Commanding Officer

58

more than a mile. Then he raised his arm above his head, which was the signal that had been arranged for the attack to be commenced.

The six top machines immediately turned to the right and dived steeply in the direction of the enemy balloons.

Biggles, with Algy at one wing-tip and the Professor at the other, turned slightly to the left, and then came round on his original course to watch the bottles go overboard. He pushed up his goggles and rocked with silent mirth as the six Camels, with the Fokkers now in hot pursuit, began heaving their curious cargo overboard.

'My hat! That's the funniest thing I ever saw in my life!' he chuckled.

The six machines, with the Fokkers still behind them, were soon mere specks in the sky, far away and below them. He banked steeply towards the balloons, and, raising his left arm above his head, pushed the control-stick hard forward.

The Camel stood on its nose and roared down in a wire-screaming dive with Algy and the Professor close behind. The sausages seemed to float up to meet them. Not a single burst of archie (anti-aircraft gun-fire) stained the sky. The plan had worked.

Biggles took the centre sausage in his sights, and grabbed his gun-lever.

At three hundred feet two streams of orange flame leapt from the twin Vickers guns on his engine cowling as he pumped lead into the ungainly gasbag.

'Got him!' he grunted, with satisfaction, as a streamer of black smoke burst out of the side of the victim.

59

He held his fire a fraction of a second longer, then pulled up in a steep zoom, glancing backwards as he did so. A triumphant yell burst from his throat, but it gave way to a mutter of annoyance. Two of the sausages were falling in flames; the other was still intact, but it was not that which had provoked the exclamation.

The Professor had evidently missed and had turned back for a second attack. Biggles grinned as he saw the flames light up the side of the third balloon.

Simultaneously an inferno of darting flames and smoke tore the air around him. He dived for the Line, looking anxiously ahead for the Fokkers as he did so. There they were, all ten of them, coming back.

'This isn't going to be so funny!' he muttered between set teeth, as he watched the ten enemy tri-planes streaking down out of the blue with the speed of light on a course that would intercept them before they could reach the Lines and safety.

He beckoned to Algy to come closer, pointing towards the enemy machines, and Algy obediently crept in close against his wing-tip. Where was Henry? Biggles' brow puckered in a frown as he scanned the sky in every direction, but could see no trace of him.

If the Fokkers caught him alone, he would stand a poor chance of ever getting back.

There was no time for further meditation, for the Fokkers, painted all colours, were falling on them like a living rainbow. Biggles tilted his nose up a trifle and took the leader, who was flying a blue machine, in his sights.

At five hundred feet the enemy formation broke like a bursting rocket, each machine swerving round to attack from a different direction. Biggles paid little attention, for his eyes—the mirth gone from them now—were fixed on the Spandau guns on the nose of the blue machine.

Through the gleaming swirl of his prop he saw two streaks of stabbing flame leap from them, and his hand closed on the gun lever on his own control-stick. Something crashed against his ring-sight with a shrill metallic whang.

His windscreen disappeared as completely as if it had been swept away with a blow from an axe; an invisible hand snatched at the shoulder of his coat, but he did not flinch. He was watching his own tracer bullets boring into the engine of the blue machine.

Only when collision seemed inevitable did the German pilot lose his nerve and swerve, and Biggles whirled round on his tail in the lightning right-hand turn for which the Camel was famous. A red machine with yellow wheels swept past, with Algy glued to its tail, but two other triplanes were close behind.

The blue machine roared up in a perfect stalling turn, but even as Biggles took it in his sights an ominous flack, flack, flack warned him that an unseen enemy was perforating his fuselage.

Out of the corner of his eye he saw two triplanes meet head-on and break up into fragments in a sheet of flame. The sight left him unmoved, for he had seen it happen before. Another machine roared past him, leaving a long plume of black smoke in its wake as it plunged headlong to oblivion, but it was gone before he could see whether it was friend or foe. Coloured machines flashed across his sights, and his guns chattered incessantly.

'This won't do!' he muttered anxiously, flinging the Camel into a steep bank to survey the position. 'We'll be out of ammunition in a couple of minutes at this rate.'

Algy was still on the tail of the red Fokker, which had also gone into a steep bank in an effort to escape him. The other machines followed, and a moment later they were all whirling around in an ever-decreasing circle.

Where was Henry? Biggles wished he knew, for his absence worried him. Perhaps he had slipped home before the dog fight started, and Biggles hoped fervently that such was the case.

Meanwhile, the position of the other two Camels was desperate, and he said bitter things about the other six Camels, which, having got rid of their bottles, had evidently gone straight on home without waiting to see whether the three balloon-strafing machines had got clear.

A V-shaped formation of nine tiny dots far overhead caught his eye, and he laughed hysterically as he recognised them for British S.E.5's. 'That's Wilks and his crowd!' he told himself delightedly. 'Raymond has sent them over here to get the sausages. They've arrived too late, but they are just in time to help us out of this mess.'

The S.E.s were coming down, still in formation, in an almost vertical dive, but the Huns had seen them, too, and one by one they broke out of the circle and dived for home. Biggles did not pursue them, as he had little ammunition left and felt that they could now safely be left to the S.E.s.

Wilks, in his blue-nosed machine, roared by, placing his thumb against his nose and extending his fingers in the time-honoured manner as he passed the Camel. Biggles grinned, and returned the salute in like manner.

'Lor! What a day!' he chuckled, as he raced towards

the Lines for safety. 'I should like to see old Wilks' face when he sees we've knocked all those sausages down!'

Once more his eyes swept the skies. Over Duneville the air was black with archie, the gunners having evidently recovered from the bottle scare. And Wilks and his crowd, having driven the Fokkers to earth, were dodging through the barrage on their way home.

In front of him, Algy's Camel was already across the Lines. But of Henry there was no sign. Perhaps he was home already—perhaps going back another way. Anyhow, it was useless to go back and look for him.

He dived across the Lines, followed by a trail of raging archie. Six machines were taxi-ing in as he reached the aerodrome. Another was just landing.

'Have you seen Henry?' yelled Biggles to Algy, who was standing up in his cockpit, grinning, as he taxied in.

'No,' Algy said. 'I didn't see anything except Fokkers after they turned back on us. He must have been crazy to have another go at that sausage after missing it first time. Why Mac and Mahoney didn't have the sense to come back after the triplanes, I don't know. They might have known we should run into the whole bunch of them. My machine's shot to bits. My word, that red Hun could fly!'

A group of wildly excited pilots gathered around the Squadron Office, waiting to make out combat reports, and a babble of laughing voices rose into the air.

'I wish that kid'd come in,' said Biggles, with a worried frown. 'I wonder what he can be up to.'

The telephone in the office rang shrilly, and Biggles hurried to the door as he heard 'Wat' Tyler, the

Recording Officer*, speak. Wat was writing down a message, repeating it as he wrote.

'Yes,' he was saying. 'Observation Post 19—117 Brigade Royal Field Artillery.' He glanced up at Biggles and looked quickly down again. 'Yes,' he went on, 'three enemy balloons—seen to fall—just behind—enemy Front Line trenches. Yes, I've got that. One Sopwith Camel—also seen—to fall—in flames—message ends. Good-bye.'

Dead silence fell upon the group. Biggles leaned for a moment against the doorpost, staring at the ground. The knuckles of the hand that gripped his flying-cap had turned very white.

His nostrils quivered once, quickly. He looked up mistily, and his face twisted into a semblance of a smile.

'Come on, chaps!' he said huskily. 'Let's aviate!'

---

* The officer designated to supervise the collection of all squadron records.

Chapter 5
The Trap

Beating time with his left hand on the side of the cockpit of his Camel plane, Biggles hummed an inaudible tune as he cruised along sixteen thousand feet above Le Cateau, on patrol.

Looking forward over the leading edge of his lower port plane, he could see an R.E.8, ten thousand feet below. The British plane was beetling round and round in a monotonous circle as it signalled the results of their shooting to the gunners on the ground. A winding trail of black archie smoke marked its erratic course.

The eyes of the Camel pilot instinctively lifted and probed the sky above for prowling enemy scouts who might have designs on the artillery plane. He squinted carefully between outstretched fingers in the direction of the sun, and then, satisfied that all was well, swung round in a wide circle in the direction of Duneville.

His roving eye fell on a moving speck three thousand feet above, heading towards the British Lines. Its twin tail-plane showed it to be a German Hannoverana, and he altered his course to overtake it. But the German observer was wide awake, for the black-crossed enemy machine turned instantly and raced nose down for its own side of the Lines.

Biggles watched its departure sombrely, knowing full well that with its advantage of height he could not catch it. 'I wish they'd put some men in their kites who'd stop and fight!' he complained bitterly, as he returned to his original course.

Approaching Duneville, still humming, he leaned far out of the cockpit and studied the atmosphere below intently. An object far below caught his eye, his tune ended abruptly, and his left hand remained poised in mid-air.

'If that isn't another blinkin' sausage!' he muttered. 'Those boys deserve to succeed. I seem to spend my life shooting down sausages over Duneville!'

He edged a little nearer the enemy sausage snatching swift, anxious glances above and behind him.

'No escort, eh?' he mused. 'That's odd!' He throttled back, and still keeping well away from the kite balloon, began gliding down in a wide circle. He could see the two occupants now, bending over the edge of the basket studying the ground below.

Like a fish approaching a bait, ready to dart away at the first sight of danger, he side-slipped a little nearer the object of his curiosity.

'No archie, eh?' he muttered. It was amazing to him that there should be no archie directed at him by the enemy. 'That's funnier still. What sort of a balloon is this, anyway?' He turned his eyes again to the observers in the basket. 'You'll get a stiff neck, you two, if you stand there like that much longer!' he said sarcastically.

He watched the sausage for some minutes with intense interest, wondering whether he should risk an attack, and then a curious expression crept slowly over his face. The observers in the basket were still in the same position. Indeed, they had not moved since he had first seen them.

There was something unnatural in the way they

stared steadfastly into space without even troubling to glance in his direction.

Suddenly he fixed them with a long, penetrating stare, and then, catching his breath sharply, opened his throttle wide and raced away in the direction of the Lines.

Without warning, a furious bombardment of archie broke out around him, but he only laughed as he dodged and twisted through the pungent black smoke and twinkling stabs of orange flame.

A few minutes later he landed at Maranique, switched off his engine, and after a curt 'She's flying perfectly' to his fitter and rigger, strode quickly in the direction of the officers' mess. The five or six officers who were in the room looked up as he entered.

Biggles' eyes swept over them and came to rest on MacLaren, who, with three others, was playing bridge at a table near the far window.

'Who's in the air, Mac?' Biggles asked.

'Mahoney's out on patrol, with a couple of new men. Why?' Mac replied.

'Which way have they gone, do you know?'

'No idea, but they're due back any minute. Hark! Here they are now,' Mac added, glancing through the window to where three Camels were gliding in over the sheds.

Biggles crossed to the fireplace, lit a cigarette, and waited until the three pilots entered.

'Listen, everybody!' he called. 'There's a new kite-balloon up at Duneville. Don't anybody go near it!'

MacLaren looked at him in astonishment.

'Why?' he cried, 'what's biting you? Have you bought it, or something?'

'You'll buy it if you go near that kite!' answered Biggles grimly.

'What's wrong with it?' MacLaren demanded.

'I don't know—yet. But whatever it is, it isn't nice, you can bet your boots on that. Hold hard a minute!' Biggles walked quickly to the hall and took up the telephone.

'287 Squadron, please—and make it snappy,' he told the telephone operator. 'Oh, hallo, Freddy!' he called, a moment later. 'Is Wilks there?' Another pause, and then: 'Is that you, Wilks? Fine! Listen, laddie. There's a new kite up at Duneville. It looks like one of the old obsolete Parseval-Drachen type, so they must be running short of balloons. But there's more to it than that.

'What's that? You know all about it? I'll bet you don't. I've rung you up to tell you to keep away from it. What? No, it isn't mine, and I don't want it, either. You can have it. Serious, there is something fishy about that kite—what's that?—just gone off to get it—who did you say? Young Tom Ellis? Oh! I'll try to stop him. Cheerio!'

Biggles slammed the receiver down, and without looking to right or left ran through the ante-room and down the tarmac to where he had left his Camel.

Two minutes later he was in the air, flying back over the course by which he had returned less than a quarter of an hour earlier. He tore across the trenches at five thousand feet, and zigzagging his way through the Line archie, he raced full-out for the Duneville balloon.

Two miles away, and a mile above him, he spied the S.E.5, piloted by young Tom Ellis, which he was trying to head off, and he muttered under his breath as he realised at once that he could not catch it. From a

68

distance of less than a mile he witnessed the whole tragedy from start to finish.

He saw the S.E flash around, put its nose down almost vertically towards the lazily floating gasbag, and then zoom up over it at the end of its dive. As the S.E. drew level with the top of the balloon there was a blinding flash of flame.

A great cloud of smoke appeared in the air where the balloon had been, and even at the distance he was from it, Biggles felt his machine rock to the 'bump' as the blast of the explosion struck it.

With staring eyes and set, white face, Biggles watched pieces of debris fall earthwards from the smoke—a wingless fuselage, wheels, broken pieces of wood and torn fabric.

He waited to see no more, but raced back again to the aerodrome. He flung the door of the squadron office open without knocking, and fixed 'Wat' Tyler, the Recording Officer, with a hostile stare.

'Where's the old man?' he snapped.

'In the mess. Why?' Tyler answered.

'Don't ask why! Give me that 'phone. 287 Squadron—and jump to it,' he told the operator tersely. 'I want Captain Wilkinson, please.' Then, a moment later: 'Hallo, is that you, Wilks? It's all over—they got him—blew the poor little beggar to dust as he went over. There must have been a ton of ammonal in that basket along with two dummy figures! Yes—see you later!'

Ignoring Tyler's 'What was it, Biggles?' he walked slowly down the tarmac to the ante-room. All eyes were turned on him as he entered. Major Mullen took one look at his face, flashed a quick glance at MacLaren,

69

then dropped his eyes again to the newspaper he was reading.

Biggles picked up a tumbler from a card-table as he passed, looked at it intently for a minute, and then hurled it with all his force at the fireplace. It struck the chimney-piece with a crash. Splinters of glass flew in all directions. No one moved. No one spoke. Major Mullen did not even look up.

Biggles kicked the table out of his way with a snarl that was half a sob, flicked a pack of cards into the air with a vicious sweep of his gloves, crossed to the fireplace, and, resting his head on his arms, stared with unseeing eyes into the grate.

'I hear 207 are getting Snipes,' observed the major casually to MacLaren.

'Good! Maybe we'll get 'em soon,' replied MacLaren. 'Have a drink, Biggles?' he added, reaching for the bell.

'Not for me,' replied Biggles in a low voice, and then, after a short pause: 'They've got young Tom Ellis. I was with the kid in Amiens last night—Well, why don't you say something, somebody?' he cried loudly, looking around aggressively.

'They blew him to bits with a load of high explosive,' he went on, through set teeth. 'They couldn't get him any other way, the dirty, underhanded hounds—' His voice rose to a shrill crescendo and he stamped his foot on the floor. He broke off suddenly and started towards the door.

'Hold hard, I'm coming!' cried Algy.

'Stay where you are!' snarled Biggles, thrusting him aside. He went out and slammed the door.

'What's he going to do, sir?' asked Algy, white-faced, turning to the C.O.

70

Major Mullen ignored the question. 'Which way has he gone, Mac?' he asked quickly, hurrying towards the window.

'Down to the sheds,' replied the flight-commander.

'What's he going to do, sir?' cried Algy again, his lips trembling.

'I'll tell you what he's going to do,' answered the major heavily, going back to his chair and picking up the newspaper he had dropped. 'He's going over the German Lines, and he'll shoot at everything that moves on legs, wheels, or wings. His machine will probably be a "write-off" when he comes back—if he does. The odds are about ten to one he doesn't.

'But it's no use trying to stop a man in that state. He's stark, staring, fighting mad. I've seen it before. If he kills somebody and doesn't get killed himself, he'll be as right as rain when he comes back.'

'I see, sir,' said Algy slowly, edging off towards the door.

'Stay where you are! Nobody will take the air until he comes back,' continued the major sharply. 'I don't want to finish off the day with only two serviceable machines in the squadron. I know what will happen if you try to follow him!' he added knowingly.

Biggles' mechanics eyed him in silent apprehension as he climbed into the cockpit of his Camel. His face was chalk-white, and his eyes blazed with the inward fire that was consuming him. He was deadly calm. Pulling his goggles down over his eyes, he waved the chocks away, and, without another glance at the wide-eyed mechanics, thrust his throttle open and raced across the turf like a bullet.

'Well, that's the last we shall see of him!' observed

71

Smyth, the flight-sergeant, gloomily. He had been in France three years, and knew the symptoms only too well—nerves stretched taut under the strain of continually facing the prospect of sudden death, until they reached the stage where it only needed a touch to snap them, leaving the owner a nervous wreck.

'Not 'im,' muttered Biggles' Cockney fitter proudly. ''E'll get 'ome all right. The 'Un ain't born as could—'

'What do you know about it?' roared the flight-sergeant. 'Get to your work, all of you!' he yelled, revealing that his own nerves were not what they once were.

Meanwhile, Biggles eyed the enemy trenches in a cold stare of hatred. They had killed Tom Ellis, poor little Tom, the lovable lad with whom he had spent the previous evening. The sight of the disaster had appalled him. It had shaken his nerves as nothing had ever done before, and although he did not know it he was perilously near a breakdown. They had killed Tommy.

Well, someone else was going to be killed now. Whether he himself was killed or not was beside the point. He did not even think about that.

The faint stammer of a gun came to his ears, and he looked down, frowning. The crew of a machine-gun on the ground had pulled their weapon out of its emplacement and were spouting a stream of lead up at him.

'Well, if you want trouble, you can have it!' grated Biggles, through set teeth. 'See how you like this!' He flung the Camel on to its nose with such a lightning dive that the machine-gunners had no time to get back to cover. A double line of tracer bullets poured into them in a continual stream from two blazing fountains on the nose of a meteor that thundered down out of the blue.

The German who was firing the other gun rose to his feet, then plunged forward like a swimmer in deep water, and lay still. Two others fell across him, and the rest flung themselves into their dugouts. But one was too late. He spun like a top, then fell in a crumpled heap across the doorway.

Biggles pulled up in a steep, climbing turn, and as he did so something detached itself from his bomb-rack— and the emplacement went up in a shower of earth, concrete, and corrugated iron.

Looking over his shoulder, Biggles regarded the result of his handiwork coldly. Something spanged against the engine cowling, and several blows like lashes from a whip struck the fuselage behind him.

Shifting his glance, he became aware that a trench was full of grey-coated figures with their rifles aimed at him, and he tore down at the trench in a fresh blaze of fury.

Straight along the trench he roared, leaving a trail of destruction in his wake, and then, without looking back, he raced low along a track that led back towards the German reserve trenches.

Rat-tat-tat-tat! Rat-tat-tat-tat—stuttered his guns as he sped along almost on the ground, shooting at every living thing he saw. A ruined village came into view, and behind it a battery of enemy field-guns, with the gunners lying resting in front of the gun-pits. His arrival created a panic that was almost comical.

With one accord the gunners sprang to their feet and made a wild dash for cover as Biggles' guns tore the earth around them. Again he pulled the bomb-toggle as he swept over the gun-pits, and without waiting to see the result he flung the Camel at a staff car that was bumping slowly along the shell-pocked road.

Neither the driver nor the officers in the back seat looked around until the rattle of Biggles' guns warned them that the low-flying machine was not one of their own. The pilot held his fire until his undercarriage wheels almost grazed the car, and as he swept over it he looked back, smiling grimly. The car was upside down in the ditch that bordered the road!

Already he was feeling better. A squadron of Uhlans* watering their horses offered the next target, but for the sake of the horses he held his fire and satisfied himself by zooming low over them. The last he saw of them was loose horses galloping wildly in all directions.

Narrowly missing the telegraph wires that ran along the side of the railway line, he turned, and grinned with satisfaction as a train came into view, steaming in the direction of the Lines. Twice he raked it from end to end with his guns before he swept round again with his hand on the bomb-toggle.

The first two bombs missed their mark, but the third caught the train fairly and squarely just behind the engine tender. The damaged coach left the rails, and the rest of the train piled up on top of it.

He chased the engine until the occupants abandoned their charge and leapt for their lives down the embankment. The loose locomotive raced on with increasing speed and ran into the siding of a small station, where it collided with the end of a stationary train which burst into flames that quickly spread to the goods yard.

The appalling scene of destruction shook even the madly angry Biggles, and for the first time since he had crossed the Lines he zoomed up and looked about him to ascertain his position.

* German cavalrymen.

74

For the first time, too, he noticed that his course was marked by a long, unbroken line of black and yellow smoke, and realised, with something of a shock, that every enemy gun within range was turned on him. He passed a critical eye over his Camel, and got another shock.

In two or three places strips of fabric were trailing out behind his planes. A flying-wire had been cut, and was vibrating against his shell-torn fuselage.

'I must be crazy!' he told himself angrily, coming to his senses with a rush, and raced back towards the Lines. A Fokker D.VII* appeared from nowhere, and he grabbed his gun-lever. Rat-tat! Two shots flashed out, that was all. Furiously he struck the cocking-handles of the guns to clear the supposed jam. And then he tried them again. Nothing happened, and he knew that he had run through all his ammunition!

Twisting and dodging like a snipe, he zigzagged towards the Lines, with the Fokker in hot pursuit.

'I must be off my rocker!' he told himself again as a burst of bullets whipped through the skylight in the centre section of the Camel. 'If I get away with this, I'll give up flying and join the R.A.M.C.**!' he muttered, in a fright.

The British trenches came into sight, and, with his wheels nearly touching the ground, he roared across so low that only a quick swerve saved him from crashing into the barbed-wire entanglements. He waved cheerfully to the Tommies who had watched his approach

---

* Very efficient German single-seater biplane fighter with two forward-firing guns.
** Royal Army Medical Corps.

with breathless excitement, and then zoomed high into the air.

'Well, that's that!' he muttered wearily as he turned towards Maranique.

Algy paced disconsolately up and down the tarmac in front of the temporary hangars. From time to time he stopped, and stared anxiously into the rapidly darkening eastern sky.

A tiny speck, far off, caught his eye, and after staring hard at it for a moment, he quickened his pace and made a signal to half a dozen air-mechanics who were lounging at the door of a hangar.

'Here he comes!' he said briskly.

'I told you 'e would, Flight,' Biggles' fitter remarked to the flight-sergeant. 'They can't get 'im. I'd like to know 'ow many 'Uns he's shot up to-day, but I bet as 'ow 'e doesn't tell us. I'll betcher there ain't a round of ammunition left in 'is guns.'

The lone Camel landed, and taxied in quickly. Algy strolled towards it, and waved cheerfully to the figure that had perched itself on the hump behind the pilot's seat.

'Good heavens!' gasped Algy, staring first at the machine and then at the pilot. 'You hurt, Biggles?' he asked quickly, noting a trickle of blood on the pilot's cheek.

'Hurt? No. Why should I be?' grinned Biggles.

'What did that to your face?' asked Algy.

'Ssh—not a word!' whispered Biggles confidentially. 'It was a mosquito. It landed on my centre section and did that.' He pointed to a gaping tear in the fabric. 'Then it sprang straight for my face. And then, because I beat it off, it went over there and did that.' Biggles

76

pointed to an inter-plane strut that was splintered for three parts of its length. 'Then it jumped on to the lower plane and did that with its feet.' The pilot pointed to a row of neat holes. 'Then—'

'Oh, don't be a fool, Biggles!' grinned Algy. 'Come and have some tea.'

Biggles leapt lightly to the ground.

'Have this machine ready for dawn to-morrow,' he told the waiting mechanics.

'It will mean working all night, sir,' observed the flight-sergeant doubtfully.

'Well, that's all right! Work all night,' replied Biggles brightly. 'There's no sense in sleeping while there's a good war like this on. I shall be working all night, too.'

'What are you talking about—working all night?' asked Algy, as they made their way to the mess.

'You wait and see,' replied Biggles darkly. 'Now, listen, Algy. If anybody wants to know where I am to-night, say you don't know. If it's anything urgent, though, you'll find me at the R.E.* Depot over at St Olave. To-morrow morning get Mac or Mahoney to take you over to Duneville—say I said so—and you'll see something you won't forget in a hurry!

'Those dirty dogs at the balloon winch think they're clever. They'll be laughing like fun to-night about the way they got young Tom Ellis. But by this time to-morrow they'll be somewhere where they can't laugh. And that won't be so funny.

'You be there at six-thirty, and wait for me to come. Push any Huns who try to interfere into the floor!'

From ten thousand feet above Duneville, Algy turned

* Royal engineers.

77

for the tenth time to stare in the direction of the Lines. He glanced at his watch. It was six twenty-five. Another five minutes and Biggles should be here, he reflected, as he edged a little nearer to Mahoney, who was leading.

'Ah, here he comes now!' Mahoney had raised his right arm and pointed down to a gleaming speck that was skimming apparently just over the ground, although he realised that the Camel was probably at two, or even three, thousand feet.

'What the dickens is he up to?' mused Algy. 'He must be crazy, flying into this archie at that height!' He saw Mahoney staring hard at the machine below them, and was not surprised when the leader dropped quickly towards the Camel.

Algy's puzzled frown gave way to an expression of extreme anxiety as the archie began to work its way closer to the low machine, although the pilot twisted and turned like a wounded bird to evade it.

The Camel was stunting now, doing a succession of half-rolls that brought it nearer and nearer to the balloon winch—the very centre of the German anti-aircraft batteries.

The flight-commander had pushed up his goggles and was gazing with a fixed expression of amazement at the antics of Biggles' Camel, for there was no doubt as to who was flying the machine below them. With a horrible feeling of helplessness, Algy turned back again to watch it.

He saw the pilot loop badly, spin, and pull out in a slow barrel-roll.

'Horrors!' gasped Algy, in a strangled voice, and stared petrified at the tragedy being enacted below.

The Camel had hung on its last roll and was flying in

78

an inverted position. The safety-strap had evidently not been fastened, for the pilot hung out of the cockpit, and then, with what seemed to be a despairing clutch at the top plane, fell out and hurtled earthwards, turning slow somersaults.

The machine had righted itself, and, with engine racing, was steering an erratic course just above the ground.

Algy went as cold as ice as the body of the pilot struck the ground. Men began to run towards it from all directions, and the archie died away as the German gunners joined in the rush to see their fallen foe.

Algy snatched a swift glance at Mahoney. The flight-commander seemed to feel his eyes on him and looked back over his shoulder, and the expression on his face haunted Algy for many a day. He turned again to the ghastly tragedy below. A crowd of forty or fifty men had gathered around the body.

What followed occurred so quickly that it was some seconds before Algy could grasp what had happened. A shaft of brilliant orange flame leapt skyward. There was a thundering detonation that he could hear above the noise of his engine, and then a blast of air nearly twisted his machine upside down.

Where the crowd had been now yawned a huge crater, surrounded by a wide circle of burnt and blackened grass on which several figures sprawled in grotesque positions. The crowd had disappeared. So had the figure of the fallen pilot. So, also, had the other Camel.

He turned again and looked at his leader. Mahoney, with a curious expression on his face, waved his hand and turned in a wide circle in the direction of the Lines.

79

Biggles was waiting for them when they landed, and the other pilots gathered around him.

'What was it?' asked Mahoney, after a moment's pause.

'A hundred and fifty pounds of high explosive wrapped up in a bag of nails inside a flying-suit, cap, goggles, flying-boots, and gloves,' observed Biggles calmly. 'Did you ever hear the saying that dead men don't bite?' he went on slowly.

Algy nodded, incapable of speech.

'Well, the next time anybody tells you that you can tell him he's a liar,' continued Biggles. 'That one did!'

Chapter 6
The Funk

Biggles, his flying kit over his arm, glanced at the sky as he made his way slowly towards the hangars. As he passed the Squadron Office, Major Mullen called out to him, and Biggles paused to listen to what the C.O. had to say.

The new fellows have just arrived, and are waiting outside the mess,' began the major. 'I've posted them to your flight. Harcourt, Howell, and Sylvester are their names. They look bright lads, and should shape well.'

'Right-ho, sir!' Biggles said. 'Have they done any flying?'

'Very little, I'm afraid,' Major Mullen replied gravely. 'But we have to be thankful for anybody now. Every squadron along the Line is screaming for replacements. Go and have a word with them, and show them the Lines as soon as you can.'

'Right, sir!' Biggles altered his course towards the officers' mess, where a tender was unloading three young officers in spotless uniforms, and their kit. They looked at Biggles curiously as he approached. Could this be the famous Captain Bigglesworth they had heard so much about; the officer who had the reputation of being one of the deadliest air-fighters on the Western Front? The man who had crossed swords with some of the best of the enemy champions?

They beheld a slim, boyish figure, clad in khaki slacks

81

and a tunic soiled with innumerable oil stains. The left shoulder of the tunic was black with oil. His feet and legs were in sheepskin boots that had once reached to the thigh, but had been cut short to the knees. The strap that bound them just above the calf had been left unfastened and flapped untidily as he walked. Over his arm he carried a leather coat, greasy beyond description, with a pair of singed gauntlets hanging from the pocket.

One of the new men started to smile, but the smile died on his lips as he raised his eyes to the pilot's face. It was pale and stern, with little tired lines round the corners of his mouth. But the eyes were clear and bright, and seemed to gaze into infinite distance as if seeking something beyond.

'All right, chaps, stand easy,' he said quietly, as they saluted. 'There is no ceremony here. I'm Bigglesworth. You've been posted to my flight. Let me know if there is anything I can do for you. Which of you is Harcourt?'

'I am,' replied a fresh-complexioned youth quickly. 'And there is one thing I am most anxious to know. Tell me, is it possible to get ants' eggs here?'

'Ants' eggs!' Biggles ejaculated. 'Did you say ants' eggs?'

'Yes –'

'But ants' eggs!' broke in Biggles, amazed. 'What in the name of goodness – '

'To feed my goldfish.'

'Goldfish!' Biggles clutched at the tender for support. 'Did you say goldfish?' he cried incredulously.

'Yes; I won one at a fair in Amiens, and I've brought him with me. He's an affectionate little chap—I've named him Percy. I've got very attached to him and

82

wouldn't like to see him starve to death. He lives on ants' eggs.'

A low moan broke from Biggles' lips.

'How do you serve 'em?' he gasped. 'Fried, poached, hard-boiled, or as an omelet?'

'No, just plain, you know,' replied Harcourt brightly.

'You've made a mistake, son!' muttered Biggles. 'This is an aerodrome, not an aquarium. And what have you brought?' he went on icily, turning to Howell. 'A cage of white mice, or something?'

Howell laughed, and shook his head.

'What about you, Sylvester? Which have you got—a box of silk-worms, or a canary? Now, listen, you fellows,' Biggles went on, becoming deadly serious. 'This isn't a zoological gardens, although you'll find there are plenty of wild beasts about, waiting to bite a piece out of your ear if you give 'em half a chance. How many flying hours have you done on Camels, Harcourt?'

'Eleven and a half, sir.'

'Never mind the "sir" when you're on the tarmac. How about you, Howell?'

'Ten hours.'

'And you, Sylvester?'

'Fourteen.'

Biggles looked at the ground moodily for a moment before he spoke.

'All right,' he said tersely. 'Now, I want you to listen carefully to what I say, and remember it's for your own good. You've got to realise that when you get over the Line you'll have to fight men who have done five hundred hours' flying. I don't want to put the wind up you, but you've got to know what you're up against.

'I've had some good lads in this flight since I came

83

out, but one by one they've gone topsides*, and my own turn can't be far off. But that doesn't matter; I've had a good run, and everybody gets it sooner or later. You can't last for ever at this game, but it's up to you to last as long as you can.

'If you can get just one man before you go, you break even with the enemy—you've done your bit and it's all square. If you can get two Huns—Germans—before you go, you're one up on the enemy, and you've helped to win the war for England.

'Your toughest time will be your first week, because it will all be new and strange to you. Algy—you'll meet him in a minute—has been here six weeks, and he can call himself a veteran. I don't want to hurt your feelings, but he is more useful to me to-day than twenty men like you.

'You see,' he went on, 'air fighting is a knack—an art, if you like—that you can't learn at home. The first time you try to ride a bike you're all over the place; it's the same with swimming. And it's the same with scrapping in the clouds. It's a case of the survival of the fittest, and you've got to understand that the air over the Lines is swarming with men who know the game from A to Z.

'To send you over the Line alone, now, would be like committing murder. Well, we're going to fight them, and I'm going to show you how. But we're going to do some flying first. We are going to do six hours' flying a day for three days—two hours' formation, two hours' fighting practice, and two hours' gunnery.

'It's no use being able to fly if you can't shoot. Then I'm going to take you over the Lines, and we'll see what we can do—Hallo, who's this?' he broke off.

* Slang: been killed.

84

A hum, which rapidly became a roar, filled the air, and a moment later a Camel plane swung into view.

'Oh!' said Biggles. 'It's Algy—just watch him. I've taught him to do this at least once a day since he joined my flight, and I'm going to make you do the same thing. Now watch!'

As the Camel reached the far side of the aerodrome it suddenly stood on its nose, and a stream of tracer bullets poured from its guns. A small object on the ground sprang into the air, and trundled along for some yards. The Camel pilot cut his engine, turned, and sideslipped neatly in to a tarmac landing.

'That's a petrol tin on the ground over there,' explained Biggles, 'and Algy knows he's got to hit that—if he's got any ammunition left—before he lands. At first, it used to take him half an hour, but now he can usually do it first go, as you've just seen. Well, break away now, and be back here in an hour for flying. When we are in the air, keep an eye on me all the time. We aren't likely to meet any Huns over this side, but you never know.

'If I rock my wings it means Huns*. For no reason whatever, except engine failure, will anyone leave the formation. Stick to me, and I'll see you through—or we'll all go west together. Now let's go and get some grub.'

Four days later Biggles again addressed the new members of his flight.

'Well, chaps,' he said, 'we've got to do some real

---

* No planes had radio communication at this time, so signals using hands or the plane's movements were the only way to pass messages between planes.

work to-day. We are going over the Lines. Try to remember what I've taught you. Above all, keep your places, unless we get in a scrap—and remember that Algy is just above and behind you, looking after your tails. Come on!'

The five machines took off together and climbed steadily for height. At ten thousand feet, Biggles swung round in a wide turn and headed towards the Lines. Almost immediately a great black stain blossomed out in front of them—another, and another, but he ignored them.

Glancing back over his shoulder, he smiled grimly as he saw his followers hesitate instinctively as they realised that they were under fire—anti-aircraft gunfire, commonly known as archie!

He throttled back a trifle to allow them to catch up, and then waved cheerfully as they came close again.

For ten minutes he flew steadily, straight along the enemy lines, deliberately asking to be archied, knowing that the sooner the new men became accustomed to it the better. Then, satisfied that they had stood the test, he turned into the enemy sky.

His eye fell on an Aviatik* plane in the distance, and he turned again to head it off, but the enemy pilot saw them and raced nose down for home. Biggles had seen something else—something that caused him to push his throttle wide open, rock his wings, and thrust the control-stick forward for more speed.

Far over the Line a lone Bristol Fighter** was fighting an unequal battle with four enemy Albatros scouts.

* German armed reconnaissance biplane 1915–17.
** Two-seater biplane fighter with remarkable manoeuvrability in service 1917 onward with one fixed Vickers gun for the pilot and one or two mobile Lewis guns for the observer.

The Bristol pilot saw the Camels coming, and zigzagged wildly towards them, with the black-crossed enemy machines doubling their efforts to shoot him down before help arrived.

Biggles had a thousand feet of height to spare when his flight reached the conflict. Picking out a blue and yellow Albatros, he plunged into the fray. The next instant the five Camels and four Albatroses were whirling in a tight circle, each trying to get on the tail of an opponent.

Biggles zoomed up out of the fight to watch the combat, and to render help where it should be most needed. In spite of his anxiety, he smiled as he saw the Bristol turn about and come barging back into the fray, the gunner in the rear cockpit throwing him a wave of thanks as he passed.

But his smile became a frown as a Camel suddenly turned out of the fight and raced nose down towards the Lines. He recognised it for Harcourt's machine.

A Hun burst into flames, and another Camel was spinning earthwards. Another Hun flung itself on the tail of a third Camel, and remained there in spite of the Camel pilot's frantic efforts to throw him off.

Biggles tore down to the rescue. The Boche pilot saw him coming, and twisted to avoid the double stream of tracer bullets that leapt from the British pilot's guns; but he was too late.

The Albatros zoomed high into the air with a quick jerk, an almost certain sign that the pilot had been hit. It slipped on to its wing from the top of the zoom, and then spun dizzily. The remaining two Albatroses streaked for home.

'That'll do for to-day!' thought Biggles, as he waved the rallying signal. Algy joined him at once. Presently

87

Howell also joined him. That was all. One of the Camels had gone home early in the fight, and Biggles made a swift scrutiny of the ground for the one he had seen spinning, but he could not see it. With the Bristol Fighter bringing up the rear, they returned to the Lines, where, with a parting wave, the Bristol pilot left them for his own aerodrome.

The three Camels landed, and Biggles looked around the aerodrome anxiously. Harcourt's machine was standing on the tarmac with a little group of mechanics around it. He hurried towards it and saw what it was that caused the interest. A row of neat round holes had pierced the fabric just behind the cockpit.

'Is Mr Harcourt hit?' asked Biggles quickly.

'No, sir,' replied the flight-sergeant.

'Where is he?' Biggles demanded.

'I saw him go across to his quarters, sir.'

'I see!'

Biggles turned towards the squadron office, but 'Wat' Tyler, the recording officer, hurried towards him from the open doorway before he reached it.

'They've got one of your chaps,' the Recording Officer said tersely.

'Yes,' Biggles replied. 'Sylvester.'

'I've just had a call from one of our advanced artillery posts,' the recording officer went on. 'He crashed this side of the Line, badly wounded, but the M.O. thinks he might recover. They've rushed him to hospital. Get his kit packed up, will you?'

'I seem to spend half my time nowadays packing up fellows' kit,' Biggles said wearily. He turned on his heel and entered C Flight hut. Harcourt was sitting on his bed, his face buried in his hands. He raised an ashen face as Biggles entered.

'Why did you leave the dog-fight?' asked the flight-commander coldly.

'I—er—I—I—'

'Yes, I've got that. Go on, I'm waiting.'

Harcourt's face twisted with a spasm of pain. It seemed to age before the other's eyes.

'You might as well know the truth,' he blurted. 'I'm finished. I can't stand it. I'll never fly again—never—never—never!'

His voice became a hysterical scream.

'Stop that!'

Biggles' voice cracked like a whip-lash. Then he went on more quietly:

'Take it easy, kid,' he said kindly. 'You won't be the first to go home after one show over the Line. Don't sit here and brood. Take a walk—you may feel better to-morrow.'

Harcourt shook his head. His face was a picture of utter misery.

'No, I won't,' he said, and his lips trembled. 'I know myself better than you do. I'm finished. I nearly fainted with fright when that archie started, and when those bullets hit my machine I didn't know what I was doing.'

'I know what it feels like,' smiled Biggles. 'We all feel that way about it at first. Don't worry. We'll have another talk later on.'

He found Major Mullen at the door of the squadron office.

'Bad show, sir, I'm afraid,' he said apologetically. 'I've lost Sylvester, and Harcourt's no use—nerves all to bits. That only leaves me Howell of the new men. I

89

should like you to have a word with Harcourt. He's taking it badly, and it's no use keeping him here to kill himself and break up a good machine.

'Hallo, what's this?' he snapped, glancing upwards. Almost before the words were out of his mouth he had leapt towards a mobile machine-gun that pointed upwards on a stand a few yards away. 'Look out!' he yelled to the mechanics on the tarmac, and gripped the trigger.

The rattle of the gun was drowned in the roar of a Mercédès engine as a Fokker D.VII, painted bright red and yellow, dropped like a meteor out of the sky. The enemy plane flattened out over the huts and then zoomed high. At the bottom of its dive something detached itself from the machine and fell with a crash on the roof of one of the huts. Biggles sent a full drum of ammunition after the retreating Boche, threw up his hands disgustedly when he realised he had missed it, and then stared at Harcourt, who was racing towards him from the hut on which the missile had fallen, waving something aloft.

'What the deuce is it?' cried the major.

'Boots!' snarled Biggles. 'Boots! Boots—so that we can join the infantry!' The next instant he was running towards the sheds, shouting to Algy and Howell as he ran to join him in the air.

'Bigglesworth! Stop, you fool! Stop, I say!' yelled the C.O. 'That's just what they want you to do—go up! The whole crowd'll be waiting for you at the Line!'

But Biggles wasn't listening. White with fury, and quivering with rage he could not suppress, he had flung on his cap and goggles, jumped into his Camel, and, without waiting to see if the others were with him, he

90

streaked across the aerodrome in pursuit of the Hun that had offered the deadly insult. Not until he was at six thousand feet and the Line was in sight did he recover sufficiently from the blazing anger that was consuming him to look around to see if the others had followed.

Algy was at his right wing-tip, and behind he saw Howell's machine. He glanced to the left, pushed up his goggles, and looked again. Then he gasped. There was no mistake! It was Harcourt!

'The little fool! The crazy lunatic!' gritted Biggles. 'Why didn't he stay where he was? He'll collide with somebody at the first clash. I only hope it's a Hun, and not me, that's all!'

He turned his attention again to the scene ahead. The red-and-yellow Fokker, now a mere speck in the sky, was turning in a wide circle, and Biggles' eyes instinctively probed the sky above it. His lips parted in a bitter smile.

'So there you are!' he mused. 'How many? One— two—four—seven—eight, eh? Eight and one's nine. It looks as if somebody's going to get hurt to-day!'

The action was not long delayed. The enemy machines, confident of their superior strength, were turning towards the Camels, and Biggles' lips set tightly in a straight line. The heat of his fury suddenly subsided, leaving him stone cold. He didn't swerve an inch from his course, but flung his Camel at the nearest machine, and at two hundred feet gripped his gun control savagely.

He knew it was madness, this blindly rushing into combat with odds of two to one against. Even if they got two or three of the enemy machines, the Camels would be lucky to get back to the Line. Howell and Harcourt

91

hardly counted in an affair of this sort. It was he and Algy against the rest. At the back of his mind was one devouring thought—to get as many of the enemy as he could before they got him!

As he turned to chase the leading Fokker, which had swerved under his fire, he heard bullets ripping through the fuselage behind him, but he ignored them. There was no time for tactics. Kill or be killed was the motto of to-day!

The dog-fight became a delirium of whirling machines, zooming, rolling, and banking, firing and firing again through a network of tracer bullets. Machines flashed across his sights, and his guns chattered incessantly. With a grunt of satisfaction, he saw two Fokkers collide and fall, spinning, a tangled mass of splintered struts and fabric.

A Camel roared past in a sheet of flame, missing him so narrowly that his heart stood still. Another Fokker shed its wings as it pulled up in a vertical zoom at terrific speed, the fuselage falling like a stone through space.

A red-and-yellow Fokker—the one that had dropped the boots—roared past, zigzagging wildly, with a Camel glued to its tail, and even Biggles, hardened air-fighter as he was, caught his breath at the fury of the Camel's attack. He even risked a pause to watch it, for it seemed that the Camel was deliberately trying to ram its opponent.

The enemy pilot evidently thought so, too. For, far from trying to return the attack, he was throwing his machine about in a panic, in a vain endeavour to shake himself clear of the mad pilot who had singled him out for destruction at any cost.

Never in all his experience had Biggles seen such a sight, and it did not occur to him for one moment that the pilot in the attacking machine could be anyone but Algy. The end came suddenly. The Camel's guns spurted death at point-blank range, and the Fokker went to pieces in the air.

The victor zoomed high, and Biggles stared in stupefied amazement as he recognised the number of Harcourt's machine. He looked around the sky. Five Fokkers were retiring back over their own Lines. Only two Camels were left. He and Harcourt were alone in the sky. Four machines were smoking on the ground below.

Turning back towards the Lines, Biggles made out another Camel, very low, just gliding across to safety. He looked around again for Harcourt, and rapped out a startled ejaculation as he saw him in hot pursuit of the five Fokkers.

'He's barmy! The shock has sent him off his rocker!' muttered Biggles, as he raced after the other machine. Catching it, he had to wave frantically and almost ram the other pilot in order to make him turn. Harcourt waved his fist furiously, and reluctantly followed Biggles back towards the aerodrome.

Biggles breathed a sigh of relief as he picked out Algy's machine, standing on its nose among the shellholes around the reserve trenches, the pilot standing unharmed beside it.

'Got his engine shot up, I expect,' muttered Biggles, as he glided down towards the now visible aerodrome. 'Must have been poor Howell I saw going down.'

Landing, he climbed out, and, wiping oil from his face with his sleeve, looked earnestly at Harcourt, who had also landed and was walking slowly towards him. On Harcourt's face was an expression of utter gloom.

'What came over you?' asked Biggles, smiling.

'Came over me?' replied Harcourt. 'Did you see me knocking the spots of the red-and-yellow hound?'

'I should say I did!' said Biggles. 'I thought you'd gone off your rocker—trying to ram him!'

'I was!' Harcourt muttered.

Biggles started.

'What's that?' he said quickly.

'I'd made up my mind to get him somehow,' replied Harcourt harshly. 'I'd shot nearly all my ammunition at him without hitting him, and I thought it was the only thing I could do to get him. I'd made up my mind I was going to get him—somehow. I've never been so angry with anyone in my life before.'

'But why—why the yellow-and-red fellow in particular?' asked Biggles.

Harcourt looked up quickly, his eyes glinting with anger.

'Didn't you see what he did?' he asked in surprise.

'Yes—I saw him throw the boots,' admitted Biggles.

'Boots!' Harcourt hooted. 'I didn't care two hoots about the boots. It was where he threw them that made me so angry. They went through the roof of my hut and landed on the table beside my bed. Look!'

He groped in his pocket and held out his hand, on which lay a stripe of something golden—something that shone brightly in the sun.

'What is it?' asked Biggles, with a puzzled frown.

Harcourt tried to speak, but the words seemed to stick in his throat.

'Percy!' he said huskily. 'Poor little Percy!'

Biggles leaned against the fuselage of his machine and laughed weakly.

'It's nothing to laugh about!' snarled Harcourt. 'He

94

was swimming in his jam-jar on the table as good as gold. The boots caught him fair and square, and flattened him out like a common plaice—poor little beggar!

'I tell you, Bigglesworth, when I saw he was dead I was so angry I made up my mind to get his murderer, even if it cost me my life. It cured me of being afraid of Huns. A man is a coward who will do a thing like that!

'Let's do some more flying. *I'll teach the hounds to go about killing goldfish!*'

Chapter 7

The Professor Comes Back

Algernon Montgomery burst into the officers' mess of No. 266 Squadron.

'Biggles!' he yelled. 'Listen, everybody! The Professor's O.K.! He's down over the other side!' The words fairly tumbled out of his mouth. 'It's a fact!' he went on breathlessly. 'A message has just come through from Wing that the Boche have reported him a prisoner of war. What do you know about that?'

Biggles had sprung to his feet at Algy's first shrill announcement.

'What!' he cried incredulously. 'Say that again!'

'It's true enough. Or how would the Boche know his name?' cried Algy excitedly.

Biggles grinned and scratched his head.

'Well, I'm dashed!' he said. 'But there! Plenty of people have been shot down in flames and got away with it. If he was flying fairly low, he might have managed to sideslip down and crash on his wing-tip*. Well, well, would you believe it!'

Major Mullen hurried into the room.

'Have you heard the news, Bigglesworth?' he called.

---

* No parachutes were carried by British aircraft during this war so to jump from a plane meant certain death. Some German airmen were issued with parachutes in 1918 but the British authorities were thought to believe that issuing parachutes to their men would encourage cowardice!

96

'Young Henry Watkins wasn't killed, after all! He's down, over the other side!'

'Yes, sir,' replied Biggles. 'Algy has just told us. That reminds me of something. I wonder—I wonder!' he mused, a thoughtful frown coming over his face.

'Wonder what, Biggles?' broke in Algy impatiently. 'Come on, don't keep us in suspense!'

'The Professor being a prisoner of war reminds me of something, that's all. Listen! You know how he was always bursting with ideas? Well, he said to me one day that he wondered why on earth some organisation wasn't started to pick up British officers who had escaped from prison in Germany, at some pre-arranged rendezvous.

'You remember the lecture we had from that chap—I forget his name—who came round all the squadrons telling us what to do if we were captured? He told us about double frontiers, frontier guards, electrified wire, dog patrols, the difficulty of swimming the Rhine, and so on. Well, I sat next to Henry, and after the lecture he asked the bloke some questions about it.

'The chap said it wasn't actually so difficult to get out of prison as it was to get back through the Lines or across the frontier. That was where most people were nabbed again. Henry asked him why we didn't have some meeting-place fixed—some field where machines could go over and pick prisoners up.

'The chap said the idea had been thought of, but the trouble was there were so many German spies over this side that the enemy would know which fields were to be used as soon as we had fixed them, and the first machine that went over and landed would probably

97

find an armed guard waiting for it; or else they would wire the field* and crash the plane as it landed.

'Instead of getting a prisoner back, we should probably lose another officer and a machine as well. The idea stuck in Henry's mind, though, and he told me one evening that he reckoned we should all work in pairs within the squadron, each pair to fix up its own rendezvous. In fact, he showed me the field he had fixed on, where he would make for if he was a prisoner and escaped.

'He said we should know if he was there because he'd try to keep a small smoke-fire going in a corner of the field. As a matter of fact, there are plenty of fields close together in that locality that would do—along the east side of the Langaarte Forest. This news that he is a prisoner made me wonder if he has managed to get away and get to the field. Dash it, he might be there now! He'd get out of prison somehow! He wouldn't be in quod five minutes without working out some scheme – '

Colonel Raymond's car, from Wing Headquarters, pulled up outside, and a moment later the staff officer entered the mess. He nodded cheerfully to Biggles and the other officers, then crossed over to Major Mullen, standing near the fireplace. Presently Major Mullen beckoned to Biggles and to MacLaren and Mahoney, the other flight-commanders.

'The Colonel wants to know why you haven't found that new Boche night-bombing squadron,' began the C.O. earnestly. 'It's getting serious. They are coming

---

* To prevent fields or open spaces being used by enemy aircraft a trip wire was suspended above the ground to snag the undercarriage wheels and crash the aircraft.

over every night and doing a terrible lot of damage in back areas!'

'Don't we know it!' snorted Biggles. 'We've had an alarm every night this week. I'm getting an old man for want of sleep. No, sir, I can't spot their aerodrome, and that's a fact. I've searched every inch of the ground for forty miles. The only thing I can think of is they might be using those abandoned sheds which were used by the Richthofen crowd before they moved nearer the Line.'

'No, they're not there,' replied the colonel, shaking his head.

'How do you know that?' asked Biggles quickly, with a frown.

Colonel Raymond overlooked the breach of respect.

'We know, that's all,' he replied quietly. 'We have our own way of finding out these things!'

'I see,' answered Biggles slowly. 'Sorry!'

'Well, they're in your sector somewhere,' declared the colonel, 'and it's up to you fellows to find them. They're Friedrichshafens*, so they're big enough to see; the Boche can't hide 'em in a cowshed. Well, get busy, you fellows. I shall expect to hear from you. Good-bye!'

Biggles gazed after the retreating figure thoughtfully. 'You'll go on expecting, if I know anything!' he muttered. 'The Boche have got a nice little dug-out for those planes where they won't be disturbed. But I suppose we shall have to have another look for them.

'What about the Professor, though? Who's game to come with me to see if Henry's lit his bonfire? It must be six weeks since he went down. If he isn't there yet, we'll keep an eye on the place to see if he arrives. What

_____
* A German twin-engined biplane bomber with a crew of three.

99

about having a look this afternoon? It's some way over the Line, so the more of us there are, the merrier!'

'I'm game!' replied MacLaren at once. 'I'll bring my boys.'

'And I,' grinned Mahoney. 'We'll all go—the whole bunch of us!'

'Fine!' replied Biggles. 'Algy!' he called. 'Harcourt! Stand by for patrol at four-thirty. We're going to fetch the Professor home!'

'You're as crazy as he was!' growled Algy, but his twinkling eyes belied his words.

'Half a minute, what's the plan?' inquired Mahoney.

'I think the best thing to do is simply to fly over and find out if he's there, before we do anything else,' suggested Biggles.

'Suppose he is, what then?' asked MacLaren.

'Then we'll come back and decide what to do about it. We don't want to attract too much attention, though. I'll take Algy and Harcourt, and stay at about five thousand feet up. You, Mac, come along just behind me at seven or eight thousand. And you, Mahoney, bring the rest along at about ten thousand. We'll fly straight over there and back, and take no notice of anything or anybody. Come on.'

Ten minutes later nine Camel planes were roaring steadily towards the Lines in the positions which had been agreed upon. Biggles, with Algy at his right wing-tip and Harcourt at his left, settled himself comfortably in his cockpit for a fairly long cruise ahead. They raced through the archie—anti-aircraft gun-fire—over the Line, and sped on into enemy country, keeping a watchful eye open for hostile scouts.

Once a formation of half a dozen enemy Fokker tri-

100

planes appeared on the horizon and stood towards them, but spotting the other Camels high overhead the Germans thought better of it, and beat a hasty retreat.

A long straight road bordered with straggling poplars loomed up ahead, and ran like a silver thread into the blue distance, where it disappeared into the vast Forest of Langaarte, which lay like a great stain across the landscape. Biggles altered his course a trifle as he drew nearer, then began to swing round in a wide circle that would take him over the edge of the forest and the field of Henry's choice.

He pushed up his goggles and stared down intently, although he was still too far off to pick out the details of the objective field. From time to time he looked around, and a puzzled frown puckered his brow.

'Funny, no archie,' he mused, 'and this area used to be stiff with it. They must have shifted it nearer to the Lines!'

The complete absence of archie aroused his suspicions without his being able to say why. It was not normal, that was all. And anything of an unusual nature in the sky of France at that time was in itself a cause for suspicion. Again he peered downwards, then caught his breath with a little hiss of surprise. In the far corner of a long rectangular field which bordered the forest a tiny pillar of pale-blue smoke rose almost perpendicularly in the still evening air.

'He's there,' Biggles told himself unbelievingly, for, in spite of the object of their flight, he did not in his heart of hearts really expect to find that the Professor had been able to keep his word. He turned his head and looked at Algy, pointing downwards as he did so. Algy raised his thumb to show that he understood.

For a moment Biggles was tempted to risk a landing,

but the sun was already sinking in the west, throwing long, purple shadows across the ground. His impatient spirit craved for the excitement of the rescue, but the sober voice of prudence warned him to wait.

'If he's there now, he'll still be there to-morrow,' he reflected, and then, suddenly making up his mind, he headed back towards the Lines.

'Well, what do you know about it, eh?' he cried to the other flight-commanders half an hour later as they climbed out of their cockpits.

'The point is, what are we going to do about it?' muttered Mahoney seriously. 'Landing is going to be a thundering risky business. Quite apart from the risk of a trap, it only needs a rabbit hole to trip your machine up, and then where are you?'

'You leave that to me,' said Biggles confidently.

'What luck?' cried Major Mullen, hurrying from the squadron office.

'He's there!' replied Biggles. 'This is my idea, sir. We'll all go over to-morrow morning at the first glimmer of dawn, just like we did to-day, except that we'll keep a bit higher up. If the whole bunch of us start milling about the wood, low down, the entire German Army will roll up to see what's going on. So when we reach the forest, you swing away to the left, Mac, and you, Mahoney, to the right; but keep an eye on me. Algy and Harcourt will circle just above the field and keep unwanted visitors out of the way. If the Professor is there, he will have to come back on my wing.'

'Unless we ask for a two-seater to go and fetch him,' chimed in the major.

'Not likely, sir. By the time it got there, half the German Air Force would be there waiting for it. The

102

Boche know as much about what is going on this side of the Line as over their own side, and the fewer people who know about this the better. He can ride on my wing comfortably enough; I've carried a passenger that way before. As soon as I get him aboard and start off back, everybody close up round me, and we'll make a dash for the Line. How's that?'

'Suits me,' said MacLaren laconically.

'And me,' agreed Mahoney.

'That's settled, then,' said Biggles, with satisfaction.

Late that evening, Biggles threw aside the book he was reading, rose to his feet, and yawned mightily.

'Well, I'm going to roost,' he announced. 'Don't forget the show in the morning. We leave the ground at dawn, and – ' He broke off suddenly, and stiffened into an attitude of expectancy. Every officer in the room did the same.

Algy, who was thumping the battered mess piano, stopped in the middle of a bar with his hands raised. From a buzz of conversation and laughter a hush settled over the room in which a pin might have been heard to drop.

A civilian, visiting the Front for the first time, might have wondered what had caused the change of attitude, for it was by no means obvious. From the far distance came the thunder of guns along the Line. Above it, sharper detonations, also in the distance, could be heard. Every man in the room knew that it was archie, bursting high in the sky.

'Coming closer!' observed Biggles.

'Hope they aren't coming here,' grunted Mahoney.

The door burst open, and 'Wat' Tyler, the Recording Officer, dashed into the room.

103

'Get those lights out, your poor prunes!' he grated. 'Can't you hear that archie? Bombers are heading this way. Haven't you any more sense than to sit here with all the candles alight, making the place like a blinking beacon? Get 'em out—quick!'

Biggles strolled towards the door.

'I wish you wouldn't get so panicky, Wat,' he complained. 'Let's go and watch the fireworks.'

As he opened the door the noise increased a hundredfold. A few miles away the air was full of stabbing flashes of red flame and the dull rumble of powerful engines.

'They're coming over us, if they aren't actually coming here,' declared Algy. 'I'm going to find a hole!'

'It'll need to be a deep 'un if you think it's going to stop the bombs those boys carry,' grinned Biggles. 'Hold hard, I'll come with you.'

Around them on the ground complete darkness reigned. Not a glimmer of light showed anywhere on the aerodrome. Harcourt joined them a trifle breathlessly, eyes riveted upwards to the sparkling flashes now approaching with deadly certainty. A dozen searchlights were probing the sky, their long, white fingers criss-crossing and scissoring through the inky blackness. The deep '*pour-vous, pour-vous, pour-vous*' of the engines of the bombers, sinister in the distance, took on a more menacing note.

The archie-bursts were almost immediately above them now, filling the air with an orgy of sound. A brilliant white light, shedding a dazzling radiance over the whole aerodrome, appeared like magic overhead, and hung, apparently motionless. Biggles made a swift leap towards a trench that encircled the nearest hut.

'Look out,' he yelled, 'we're for it! They're dropping parachute flares*!'

A faint wail, like the whistle of an engine far away, became audible, and Biggles crouched lower in the trench.

'Here they come!' he muttered, as the wail became a howling shriek. Instinctively the airmen flinched as the missile came nearer, seeming to be falling on their very heads. A blinding sheet of flame rose in the air not far away. There was a deafening detonation, and the earth rocked.

'That's too close for my liking,' snarled Biggles, risking a peep over the parapet, in spite of the howl of more falling bombs. 'Look, they've got A Flight sheds!' he yelled. 'They're alight. They'll set ours on fire—the wind's blowing that way. Come on, chaps.' The next instant he was sprinting towards the sheds, gleaming whitely like ghosts in the ghastly glare of the flares.

Major Mullen leapt out of the door of his office.

'Turn out, everybody!' he shouted. 'Try to save the machines!'

There was a general rush towards the blazing hangars. A cloud of earth with a blood-red core leapt up not fifty yards in front of Biggles, and he was flung violently to the ground. Gasping for breath in the choking fumes of the explosive, he picked himself up and tore on again.

One glance, and he realised it was useless to try to save any of the A Flight machines, for the canvas hangar was a roaring sea of flame that cast an orange glow over the scene of destruction. B Flight hangars were also well alight, and a streak of flame was already

---

* Burning flares suspended beneath a parachute, used to illuminate ground targets at night time.

105

licking across the roof of the shed where the C Flight machines were housed. The scene was an inferno of noise and smoke in which men moved like demons.

Biggles, the perspiration pouring off his face, seized the tail-skid of his Camel and started to drag it backwards into the open. Algy, Harcourt, the flight-sergeant, and several mechanics came to his assistance, and the C Flight machines were soon well out on the tarmac. Invisible machine-guns were chattering in the darkness above, as the Boche gunners emptied their drums of ammunition into the scene of confusion. A mechanic, standing near Biggles, gave a little grunt of surprise, stared open-eyed at his flight-commander for a moment, and then dropped limply, like a garment falling from a coat-rack.

'Two men here, quick!' Biggles snapped in a voice that commanded attention. 'Get him down to the medical officer,' he yelled, turning to see how the other flights were faring. A groan broke from his lips as he saw that in spite of their efforts neither of the other two flights had been able to save a single machine. The heat was so intense that it was impossible to get within a hundred yards of them. The bombers, their work finished, were now retiring.

'Well!' observed Biggles to the others, pointing to a row of yawning craters on the aerodrome. 'I must say they've made a good job of it. They were the Friedrichshafens the colonel was talking about this afternoon.'

Major Mullen nodded, tight-lipped.

'As you say, they've made a job of it,' he replied. 'You'd better go and get some sleep. With only three machines left on the aerodrome, you look like being busy for the next few days!' he added dryly.

106

Dawn was just breaking as Biggles, with Algy and Harcourt behind him, taxied out on to the aerodrome ready to take off—no easy matter considering the bomb-torn state of the aerodrome. The sheds were still smoking, or rather the pile of charred debris which marked the spot where they had once stood.

Biggles smiled grimly as he opened his throttle, for there seemed a fair chance that the number of serviceable machines remaining in the squadron might soon be reduced from three to two. For, in spite of the catastrophe, he had resolved to make the attempt to pick up the Professor—if the Professor was indeed at the rendezvous awaiting him. That accomplished, they would then set about finding the lair of the bombers that had wrought so much mischief. The three machines took off and headed in the direction of the Forest of Langaarte.

A big formation of enemy scouts was making for the Line, but Biggles edged away into the sun and passed them unobserved. Presently the forest loomed up on the horizon, still half-concealed by layers of early morning mist. Biggles fixed his eyes on the big field expectantly.

The task on hand was one which called for speed and accuracy. The landing would have to be made swiftly and faultlessly, for it would be unsafe to leave the Camel on the ground for more than a minute; there was no telling what eyes would watch his descent. The three machines were immediately above the field now, and the leader raised his hand in a warning signal to the others that he was going down.

The roar of his engine died away as he throttled back, and the next moment the Camel was spinning viciously to the ground. Biggles pulled the machine out of its spin, snatched a swift glance below to get his bearings, then spun again.

He spun to within five hundred feet of the ground before he came out, and then, with control-stick hard over, dropped like a stone in a vertical sideslip. He levelled out and ran smoothly to earth not more than fifty paces from the edge of the forest.

'Not so bad!' he grunted, as he unfastened his safety-belt, stood up, then stared fixedly towards the still-smouldering fire in the far corner of the field. All was still. Not a soul was in sight. With a frown of disappointment, he turned casually to scan the side of the wood.

The sight that met his eyes stunned him. It was so totally unexpected that his brain refused to grasp the image reflected upon it. His jaw dropped, and a frown lined his brow as he struggled to comprehend what was happening.

Fifty yards away, snugly set in the wood and camouflaged overhead with artificial branches of unbelievable realism, were the open maws of three huge hangars. Just inside them were the indistinct outlines of a squadron of bombers. The mechanics clustered around them were staring in his direction in obvious amazement.

And that was not the worst. Racing towards him, and already half-way between the wood and the Camel, was a line of grey-clad German troops, an officer at their head, who, seeing that he was now observed, flung up his arm and blazed away with a revolver.

A bullet ripping through the 'hump' of the Camel not two inches from where Biggles' hand rested, galvanised him into feverish activity. He dropped back into his seat with a gasp and shoved the throttle open. The Camel started forward at once.

Straight ahead, a row of trees seemed to rear up to the sky; it was obviously impossible for the Camel to clear them. Biggles swung the Camel round in its own length and tore back down-wind across the field. He ducked instinctively as a volley rang out as he raced across the front of the Germans.

The tail of the Camel had lifted and the wings were taking the weight when a scarecrow of a figure leapt from the hedge and flung itself across his path to intercept him. Automatically the pilot swerved to avoid it. There was a ghastly grinding, rending crash as the wheels were swept off and the undercarriage buckled under the oblique strain. The nose of the Camel bored its way into the ground, and then, in a whirl of flying propeller splinters, the tail whipped up and over in a complete somersault.

As the Camel folded itself up about the cockpit, it seemed to Biggles as if the end of the world had come. For a moment he lay still among the debris, fighting to restore his numbed faculties, and then, with the full realisation of the catastrophe flooding his consciousness, he struggled like a madman to get free. A flying wire* had braced itself across his face, cutting his eye badly, but he felt no pain, and dropping to his knees burrowed like a rabbit under the top of the fuselage, which was now nearly flat on the ground. He just had time to get clear, fling himself sideways, and throw a protecting arm over his face as the petrol from the smashed tank reached the hot engine and exploded with a dull whoosh! Swaying from the shock, he

---

* Flying wires—particularly on biplane aircraft—help to hold the wings in position in the air. Landing wires take the weight of the wings when the aircraft is on the ground. See front cover for illustration.

snatched a glance over his shoulder. To his horror the Germans were not more than two hundred yards away, spreading out like a fan to intercept him.

'Come on! What are you gaping at?' yelled a voice near at hand.

Biggles swung round and stared in petrified amazement at the figure that confronted him. He had no time to take in the details, but in spite of the tattered jacket, tousled hair, and unkempt appearance, it was undoubtedly the Professor!

'Henry!' gasped Biggles stupidly, for in the excitement and speed of events, he had completely forgotten the original object of his quest.

'Come on, your poor prune!' cried Henry frantically. 'Run for it!' and he led the way by taking a running jump at the hedge, regardless of thorns and briars.

Biggles followed blindly, still not quite knowing what he was doing, and found himself in a large pasture nearly as large as the field they had just left. He threw up his hands in dismay, for any attempt at concealment in such an open place was out of the question.

'Back to the wood!' he cried hoarsely, but a groan burst from his lips as his eyes fell on the grey-coated uniforms between them and the only possible cover.

He became conscious of a roaring noise in his ears, and glanced upwards to ascertain the cause. A ray of hope shot through his brain as he saw two Camels circling low overhead. He had forgotten them, but now he realised that they could hardly have failed to see the tragic end of his Camel.

'Could they land? Was the field big enough?' was the thought that crowded all others from his mind. It was at once evident that they intended to try, for they were

110

even now gliding in, wing to wing, props ticking over, not twenty feet over his head. 'Come on!' he yelled to Henry, and sprinted after them.

The two Camels touched ground about a hundred yards away, and without waiting to finish their run, swung round to meet them. Panting and gasping for breath, Biggles flung himself at full length on the lower port wing of Algy's plane and gripped the leading edge firmly.

He was far too spent to speak, and could only point upwards as a signal that he was ready to leave the ground. As in a dream, he heard the Bentley rotary engine begin its strident bellow. Bump, bump, bump, went the wheels on the uneven ground, and then the machine rose into the air.

How long Biggles lay crouching in the icy slipstream near the fuselage he did not know, but it seemed like an eternity. He was too far back to see the ground over the leading edge of the plane, so it was impossible to see what was going on below. He stared ahead through the glittering white flash of the revolving propeller, wondering vaguely where they were, and whether Harcourt had succeeded in picking up the Professor.

He turned his head slowly and risked a glance at Algy, who threateningly signalled to him to lie still, and then pointed to the left. Following the outstretched finger, Biggles saw the other Camel a few yards away with the Professor crouching on the wing.

It was bitterly cold in the hundred-miles-an-hour blast of air, even in his flying kit, which he was, of course, still wearing. And he wondered whether the Professor in his tattered rags would be able to hang on long enough to reach the aerodrome.

So anxious was he, and so wrapped up in watching

111

his companion in misfortune, that the sudden stutter of a gun near at hand made him start nervously.

'Jumping fish!' he groaned. 'Now we're in a mess!'

There was another burst of fire from somewhere close at hand. The wing on which Biggles was lying vibrated suddenly, and a row of neat round holes appeared in the fabric near the tip. He half-raised himself and peered forward. Two miles away were the zigzag lines of the trenches. He screwed his head round to look at Algy, but Algy was also looking round over his shoulder.

Biggles, following Algy's eyes, caught his breath as he saw a Fokker Triplane working itself into position for another attack. The nose of the Camel dropped a little as Algy dived for the Lines, but without shaking off his pursuer. To make matters worse, two more Fokkers were coming up behind.

Biggles knew the situation was desperate, and sensed the feeling of helplessness Algy must be experiencing—to be shot at and yet be unable to return the attack for fear of throwing his passenger off his plane. Even a quick turn, Biggles reflected, was likely to fling him right off his precarious perch.

The other Fokkers were coming in now, one of them swerving to attack Harcourt's Camel. Biggles ground his teeth in rage as the first Fokker stood on its nose and streamed down on their tail, its guns spraying a double stream of lead. Then he had an inspiration. Rising slowly to his feet, he clutched the centre section strut with his left hand, and with his right groped in the cockpit for the little niche where the Very pistol was usually kept.

He grunted with satisfaction as his hand closed over

112

the butt, and he drew the short, bulky weapon from its case. He cocked the hammer with his thumb and took quick aim at the pilot in the Fokker, whom he could see peering forward through his gunsights.

Bang! The Boche pilot started violently as a glowing ball of red fire, leaving a thick trail of smoke in its wake, flamed between his wings. His head appeared over the side of the cockpit, looking up, down, and around for the source of such an unusual missile. Algy, grinning his approval of these tactics, quickly passed Biggles another cartridge. Bang! Another ball of fire, green this time, roared away astern.

The Fokker pilot, who evidently did not approve of this method of warfare—which was not to be wondered at—waited for no more, but turned quickly towards the other Camel, and Biggles nearly choked as a ball of orange fire, changing slowly to blue, sailed over the tail of Harcourt's Camel like a Roman candle. The German saw it coming, and swerved just in time.

Biggles knew what had happened. The Professor had seen his first shot, and, taking the cue, had followed suit with Harcourt's Very pistol. The three Germans were hesitating now, as if wondering how to cope with such an unusual state of affairs. Suddenly they turned and dived for home, and Biggles, peering out from under the wing to discover the reason, saw a formation of British S.E.5's approaching. The leader, catching sight of him, came nearer, and Biggles recognised the blue prop-boss of Wilkinson's machine—'Wilks' of 287 Squadron.

The unusual spectacle of two Camels in formation, each with its pilot, as he thought, riding on the wing, evidently surprised the S.E.5 pilot, for he followed them back to the aerodrome, landing close behind them. Wilkinson's face was a picture as he sprang from his seat

113

and hurried towards where Biggles and Henry were patting each other on the back.

'What's going on?' he cried, in bewilderment. 'If you want to fly two at a time, why don't you go to a two-seater squadron and do the job properly? Haven't you got enough machines to go round?'

'No!' was the reply. 'The Friedrichshafens came over last night and pretty well wiped us out. But you'd better get back, Wilks; you'll be wanted for escort duty!'

'Escort duty! Why?'

'We've rumbled where the bombers hang out! I'm going to ring up Wing right away, and if I know anything, they'll have every day-bomber within fifty miles on the job within the hour. And they'll need an escort. There won't be any forest left by dinner-time. Now I know why there wasn't any archie there!' he cried, in a flash of inspiration, turning to Algy. 'They were trying to kid us there was nothing to guard!

'By the way, Henry,' he went on, 'how did you manage to light that fire with all those Huns about?'

'Me light a fire?' cried the Professor, in amazement. 'What are you talking about? I didn't light any fire!'

'But we saw one burning!' exclaimed Biggles.

'That was the bombers' smudge-fire—wind-indicator, you poor hoot! I had only just that moment arrived at the spot, when I saw you ground-looping,' admitted Henry.

'Well, I'm dashed!' gasped Biggles. 'When we went over last night and saw a fire burning, we were sure you were there. If the Huns hadn't been there and lit a fire, we shouldn't have gone over for you to-day, and you wouldn't be here now. Well, well, as I've said before, it's funny how things pan out at this game!'

114

Chapter 8
The Thought Reader

The summer sun blazed down in all its glory from a sky of cloudless blue. Biggles, his head resting on his hands, lay flat on his back in a patch of deep, sweet-scented grass in a quiet corner of the aerodrome, and stared lazily at a lark trilling gaily far above.

The warmth, the drowsy hum of insects, and the smell of the clean earth were balm to his tired body. For since the disaster which had robbed his squadron of two-thirds of its machines he had been doing three patrols a day. New Camel planes had now arrived, however, and at the commanding officer's suggestion he was taking things quietly for a few days.

The war seemed far away. Even the mutter of guns along the Line had died down to an occasional fitful salvo. France was not such a bad place, after all, he decided, as he glanced at his watch, and then settled himself again in the grass, his eyes on the deep-blue sky.

A little frown puckered his brow as he heard the soft swish of footsteps approaching through the grass, but he did not move. The footsteps stopped close behind him.

'You taking up star-gazing?' said a voice. It was Algy's.

'I should be if there were any to gaze at. You ought to know, at your age, that they only come out at night,' replied Biggles coldly.

'You'll go boss-eyed staring up that way,' warned

Algy. 'Do you expect to see something, or are you just looking into the future?'

'That's it,' agreed Biggles.

'What's it?' asked Algy.

'I'm looking into the future. I can tell you just what you'll see up there in exactly three and a half minutes' time.'

'You're telling me!' sneered Algy. 'You mean a nice blue sky!'

'And something else,' replied Biggles seriously. 'I've been doing a bit of amateur astrology lately, and I'm getting pretty good at it. I can work things out by deduction. My middle name ought to have been Sherlock—Sherlock Holmes, you know, the famous detective!'

'Well, do your stuff,' invited Algy. 'What are you deducing now?'

Biggles yawned, and said:

'In one minute you'll see a Rumpler* plane come beetling along from the south-east at about ten thousand feet. Our people will archie him, but they won't hit him. When he gets over that clump of poplars away to the right, he'll make one complete turn, and then streak for home, nose down, on a different course from the one he came by.'

'This sun has given you softening of the brain,' declared Algy. 'What makes you think that, anyway?'

'I don't have to think—I know!', replied Biggles. 'I've got what is known as second sight. It's a gift that – '

'Come, come, Bigglesworth,' broke in another voice. 'You can't get away with that!'

Biggles raised himself on his elbow, and found him-

---

* German two-seater biplane used for general duties as well as fighting.

116

self looking into the smiling face of Colonel Raymond, of Wing Headquarters.

'Sorry, sir!' he gasped, struggling to get to his feet. 'I thought Algy was by himself.'

'All right—lie still, don't let me disturb you. I was just looking around—Hark!'

A faint drone became audible high overhead, and three pairs of eyes turned upwards to a tiny black speck heading up from the south-east. Although small, it could be recognised as a German aeroplane, a Rumpler.

Whoof! Whoof! Whoof!

Three little fleecy white clouds blossomed out some distance behind it as the British archie—anti-aircraft—gunners took up the chase.

Biggles glanced at the others out of the corner of his eye, and their expressions brought a quick twitch of amusement to the corners of his lips. His smile broadened as the Rumpler held on its way until it was almost exactly above the group of poplars to which he had referred. Then, very deliberately, it made a complete circle and raced back, nose down, towards the Lines on a different course.

'Not a bad forecast for an amateur!' observed Biggles calmly.

'Pretty good!' admitted Algy reluctantly. 'Maybe you know why he's flying in that direction now?'

'I do,' replied Biggles. 'It's a matter of simple deduction. He's going that way because if he followed his own course back he'd just about bump into Mahoney's flight coming in from patrol. He knows all about that, and as he doesn't fancy his chance with them he's steering wide of them.'

The enemy Rumpler was almost out of sight now,

117

and the drone of its engine was gradually drowned by others rapidly approaching. Following the course by which the Rumpler pilot had crossed the Lines came three British Camel planes, straight towards the aerodrome.

'I told you my middle name ought to have been Sherlock!' grinned Biggles.

'Good show, Bigglesworth!' said the colonel. 'I must say that was very neat. Tell us how you knew all this.'

'Oh, sir!' replied Biggles reprovingly. 'Fancy asking a conjurer to show you how he does his tricks! It isn't done.'

'But I'm very interested,' protested the colonel.

'So am I, to tell you the truth, sir!' Biggles replied. 'You know as much as I do now, but I figure it out this way. The average German hasn't very much imagination, and he works to a timetable, like a clock. I've been over here for the last two days at this time, and on both occasions that Rumpler has turned up and done exactly the same thing.

'Well, when I put my ear to the ground a little bird tells me that what a Hun does twice he'll do three times—and he'll keep on doing it until someone stops him. Maybe I shall have to stop him.

'If you ask me why he comes over here you've got me. I don't know. But I should say he comes over to look at something. He doesn't just come over on an ordinary reconnaissance. He's sent to look at something which he can see from that position where he turned over the poplars.

'Having seen it, he beetles off home. I may be wrong, but even my gross intelligence tells me he doesn't come over here just for fun. I must confess I'm getting a bit curious. What Huns can see I ought to be able to see.'

'That's what I was thinking,' agreed the colonel. 'The Huns seem to be seeing quite a lot of this sector, too, of late. A week ago an artillery brigade took up a position in the sunken road at Earles. They were well camouflaged and could not have been seen from above, yet they were shelled out of existence the same night. That wasn't guesswork.

'We had to have some guns somewhere, so a couple of days ago we brought up a heavy naval gun, and sank it in a gun-pit behind that strip of wood on the Amiens road. It was perfectly concealed against aerial observation, yet by twelve noon the Boche artillery were raking that particular area and blew it to pieces. That wasn't guesswork, either.

'Then some ammunition lorries parked behind the walls of the ruined farm at Bertaple—the same thing happened to them. Now you know what I mean when I say that the Boche has been looking pretty closely at this sector.'

'Someone's been busy, that's certain,' agreed Biggles.

'I wish you'd have a look round,' the colonel went on. 'I don't know what to tell you to look for—if I did, there would be no need for you to go. You'll have to put two and two together, and you're pretty good at that!'

'Don't make me blush in front of Algy, sir!' protested Biggles, grinning. 'Right-ho, I'll beetle around right away and see if I can see what the gentleman in the Rumpler saw!'

Half an hour later, Biggles was in the air flying over exactly the same course as that taken by the Boche machine, and as he flew he subjected the ground below to a searching scrutiny. Reaching the spot where the

119

Rumpler had turned, he redoubled his efforts, studying the landscape road by road and field by field.

There was a singular lack of activity. Here and there he saw small camps where British battalions from the trenches were resting. He picked out a wrecked windmill, minus its arms, an overturned lorry, and a dispatch-rider tearing along a road in a cloud of dust.

One or two small shell-torn villages came within his range of vision, and a farm labourer harvesting his corn, piling the sheaves into shocks, regardless of the nearness of the firing-line.

Shell-holes, both old and new, could be seen dotted about the landscape, but he could not see a single mark likely to be of interest to, or which might be taken as a signal for, the enemy. He saw the place where the artillery brigade had been shelled, and he turned away, feeling depressed.

For an hour or more he continued his quest, but without noting anything of interest. And then, in not too good a humour, he returned to the aerodrome.

Colonel Raymond was talking to Major Mullen when he landed.

'Well, Sherlock,' called the colonel, 'what's the latest?'

'Nothing doing, sir,' replied Biggles shortly. 'But I haven't given up hope. I hope to pass the time of day with that Rumpler pilot to-morrow, anyway!'

The following morning he was in the air in ample time to intercept the Boche machine. In fact, he had deliberately allowed himself a wide margin of time in order to make a further survey of the ground which appeared to be the object of the enemy plane's daily visit, and towards which he now headed his Camel. Reaching it, he gave a grunt of annoyance as his pro-

120

bing eyes searched the earth below. Everything was just the same—the same lonely farm labourer was still harvesting his corn.

Flying lower, he saw, farther on, a large body of British troops—a brigade, he judged it to be—lying fairly well concealed along the edge of a wood, no doubt awaiting their turn to move up to the trenches.

He wondered vaguely whether the prying eyes in the Rumpler would see them, but he decided not, both from the fact that the machine would be too high up and would hardly be likely to venture so far over the British Line.

He glanced at the watch on his instrument board and saw that he still had a quarter of an hour to wait for the Rumpler, assuming it came at the same time as before.

'Well, I might as well be getting plenty of height,' he mused, as he tilted the nose of the Camel upwards, glancing down for a final survey of the ground as he did so.

His eye fell on the labourer, still working at his harvest. It seemed to Biggles that he was working unnecessarily fast, and a frown lined his brow as he looked around the sky to see if there were any signs of an impending storm to account for the man's haste. But the sky was an unbroken blue canopy from horizon to horizon.

He looked back at the man on the ground, and, leaning over the side of the cockpit to see better, he stared at the field and the position of the shocks of corn with a puzzled expression on his face.

It struck him that, in spite of the man's haste in moving the corn, the shocks were as numerous as they had been the previous day. They only seemed to have

121

moved their positions, and they now formed a curious pattern, quite different from the usual orderly rows.

'So that's your game, is it?' Biggles muttered, after a quick intake of breath, as he realised the significance of what he saw. His eyes followed a long line of sheaves pointing in the direction of the concealed infantry, and a number of isolated shocks which probably indicated the distance they were away, and so disclosed their position to the German aerial observer!

Biggles' brain raced swiftly. What should he do? There were several courses open to him. He might proceed with his original plan and shoot down the Rumpler. That would at least prevent the information from reaching the German gunners.

But suppose he failed? Suppose the Boche shot him down? He did not anticipate such a catastrophe, nor did he think it likely, but it was a possibility.

His engine might be damaged, when he would be forced to land, in which case there was nothing to prevent the Rumpler from reaching home. He might have engine trouble and have to force-land, anyway, and he shuddered to think of the consequences, for he had not the slightest doubt but that the British infantry would be annihilated by the guns of the German artillery.

Another plan would be to return to the aerodrome, ring up Colonel Raymond at Wing Headquarters, and tell him what he had discovered. The colonel could then send a message to the brigade warning them to shift their position before the bombardment started.

'No,' he decided, 'that won't do.' It would take too long. It would allow the Boche plane ample time to return home and start the enemy gunners on their deadly work before the message could reach the brigade.

The only really sure plan seemed to be to land and destroy the tell-tale signal before the Boche plane came over. If he could do that quickly he might still have time to get off again and get the Rumpler when it arrived.

'Yes,' he thought, 'that's the safest way!' There was still ten minutes to go before the Rumpler was due to appear on the scene.

Having made up his mind, he sideslipped steeply towards the ground near to where the supposed peasant was at work. The fact that he was unarmed did not worry him. After all, there was no reason to suppose that the spy would suspect he had been discovered—his method of conveying information to the enemy was so simple and so natural that nothing but a fluke or uncanny perception could detect it.

It was improbable that a roving scout pilot would even pass over the field so far behind the Lines, much less suspect the sinister scheme. But the improbable had happened, and Biggles, as he swooped earthwards, could not help admiring the ingenuity of the plan.

He did not risk a landing on the stubble of the cornfield, but dropped lightly to earth on a pasture a short distance away. Climbing from the cockpit, he threw his heavy flying coat across the lower wing and started off at a steady trot towards the cornfield. As he neared it he slowed down to a walk in order not to alarm the spy, and made for a gate leading into the field.

He saw the supposed labourer, dressed in the typical blue garb of a French peasant, still carrying the sheaves of corn, and he smiled grimly at his thoroughness. For the labourer did not so much as glance up when a distant deep-toned hum announced the approach of his confederate, the Rumpler.

He saw Biggles coming towards him and waved gaily.

'*Bonjour, m'sieur le capitain**!' he cried, smiling, and the pilot was too far away to see the curious gleam in his eyes.

'*Bonjour, m'sieur!*' echoed Biggles, still advancing. He was still about twenty yards away when he saw the peasant's hand move quickly to his pocket, and then up.

Before he even suspected the other's purpose, a deafening roar filled Biggles' ears, and the world seemed to blow up in a sheet of crimson and orange flame that slowly turned to purple and then to black.

As he pitched forward limply on to his face, Biggles knew that the spy had shot him!

Biggles' first conscious realisation as he opened his eyes was a shocking headache. He tried to raise his arm to his head to feel the extent of the damage done by the spy's bullet, but his arm seemed to be pinned to his side. It was dark, too, and an overwhelming smell of fresh straw filled his nostrils, seeming to suffocate him.

He saw some narrow strips of daylight in the darkness, and it took him several minutes of concentrated thought to realise that he was buried under a pile of corn sheaves.

With a mighty effort that seemed to burst his aching head, he flung the sheaves aside and rolled out into the open, blinking like an owl in the dazzling sunlight.

He struggled to his feet, and, swaying dizzily, looked about him. Apparently he was at the very spot where he

_____

* French: Good day, Captain

124

had fallen; everything was precisely the same except that the spy was nowhere in sight.

It seemed as if the spy had just flung the sheaves of corn over the pilot's unconscious body to conceal it from any casual passers-by, and then had made his escape.

Biggles wondered how long he had been unconscious, for he had no means of knowing; his watch was on the instrument board of the Camel. From the position of the sun, however, he decided that it could not have been very long, but ample for the Rumpler pilot to read the message and return. At least, the machine was nowhere in sight, and he could not hear the sound of its engine. He tried to think, raising his hand to his aching head and looking aghast at his red-stained fingers when he took it away.

Suddenly he remembered the infantry, and with a shock he recalled the perilous position in which they must now be placed. He must get in touch with the brigade, was the thought that hammered through his brain. The inevitable artillery bombardment had not yet started, and he might still be in time to save them!

The sudden splutter of a motor-car engine made him swing round, and he was just in time to see a rather dilapidated old Renault car with the spy at the wheel, disappearing out of the yard of the small farmhouse a short distance away, to which the cornfield evidently belonged.

At the same time a thick column of smoke began to rise from the farm itself, and he guessed that the spy had set fire to the place to destroy any incriminating documents or clues he might have left behind in his hurried departure.

125

Biggles' lips set in a straight line, and his eyes narrowed.

'You aren't getting away with that!' he snarled, and started off at a swaying run towards the place where he had left his Camel, breathing a sigh of relief when he saw it was still there.

He paused for an instant at a ditch to soak his handkerchief and bind it round the place on the side of his head where the spy's bullet had grazed it.

'If I ever get a closer one than that it will be the last!' he muttered grimly, as he realised what a close shave he had had. Indeed, the spy must have thought he had killed him, he reflected, or he would not have left him to tell the tale.

He climbed into the cockpit, and, after a swerving run, somehow managed to get the machine off the ground and headed towards the road down which the spy had disappeared.

He saw the car presently, and the long cloud of dust hanging in the air behind it, and he flung the Camel at it viciously, knowing that he had no time to lose.

He knew he ought to go straight to the infantry brigade and sound the warning, but his blood was up and he could not bear to think the spy might escape to continue his dangerous work elsewhere.

In any case, he thought, as he tore down the road just above the column of dust, the Rumpler pilot could scarcely have reached home yet, for the fact that he— Biggles—had caught the spy in the act of escaping indicated that he had not been unconscious for more than a few minutes.

His lips parted in a mirthless smile as he saw the fugitive look back over his shoulder at the pursuing demon on his trail, and the car leaped forward as the spy strove to escape by increasing his speed.

Biggles laughed. The idea of any vehicle on the ground leaving his Camel, which was doing 140 miles an hour, struck him as funny. But the smile gave way to the cold, calculating stare of the fighting airman as the Camel drew swiftly into range, and Biggles' eyes sought his sights.

Rat-tat-tat-tat-tat! The twin Vickers guns began their song. The end came suddenly. Whether he hit the driver, or burst a tyre, or whether it was simply the result of the driver trying to take a bend at excessive speed, Biggles did not know, nor did he stop to ascertain. The car seemed suddenly to plough into the road, and a great cloud of dust arose above it.

The bodywork, with a deliberation that was appalling to watch, seemed slowly to spread itself over the landscape. A solitary wheel went bouncing along the road. A tongue of flame licked out of the engine, and in a moment all that was left of the wreck was concealed under a cloud of smoke.

Biggles grimaced at the unpleasant sight, and circled twice to see if by some miracle the driver was still alive. But there was a significant lack of movement near the car, and he shot off at a tangent in the direction of the infantry encampment.

He made a bad landing, excusable in the circumstances, in an adjacent field, and ran quickly towards a group of officers whom he saw watching him.

'I must speak to the Brigadier at once!' he cried, as he reached them.

'Did no one teach you how to salute?' thundered an officer who wore a major's crown on his sleeve.

127

Biggles flushed, and raised his hand smartly to the salute, inwardly fuming at the delay.

'I must speak to the Brigadier or the Brigade-major at once!' he repeated impatiently.

A major, wearing on his collar the red tabs of a staff-officer, hurried up and asked:

'Are you the officer who just flew low over – '

'Do you mind leaving that until later, sir?' ground out Biggles. 'I've come to tell you to move your men at once. I – '

'Silence! Are you giving *me* orders?' cried the brigade-major incredulously. 'I'll report you for impertinence!'

Biggles groaned, then had an inspiration.

'May I use your telephone, sir? It's very urgent!' he asked humbly.

'You'll find one at headquarters—this way!' In the Brigade Headquarters, Biggles grabbed the telephone feverishly. The Brigade-Major and an orderly-officer watched him curiously. In a few moments he was speaking to Colonel Raymond at Wing Headquarters.

'Bigglesworth here, sir!' he said tersely. 'I've found what you were looking for. That Boche came over to pick up a message from a spy who has signalled to the German gunners the position of the brigade from whose headquarters I am now speaking—yes, sir—that's right—by the side of the wood about two miles east of Buell.

'Yes, I've tried to tell the people here, but they won't listen. I killed the spy—he's lying under the wreckage of his own car on the Amiens road. Yes, sir—I should say the bombardment is due to start any minute.'

'What's that—what's that?' cried a voice behind him.

128

Biggles glanced over his shoulder and saw the Brigadier watching him closely.

'Just a moment, sir,' he called into the telephone, and then, to the Brigadier: 'Will you speak to Colonel Raymond, of 51st Wing Headquarters, sir?'

The Brigadier took the instrument and placed the receiver to his ear. Biggles saw his face turn pale. An instant later he had slammed down the receiver and ripped out a string of orders. Orderlies dashed off in all directions, bugles sounded, and sergeant-majors shouted.

Ten minutes later, as the tail of the column disappeared behind a fold in the ground to the rear, the first shell arrived. A salvo followed. Presently the earth where the British camp had been was being torn and ploughed by flame and hurtling metal.

Biggles ran though the inferno of flying earth and shrapnel to where he had left the Camel. The pain in his head, forgotten in the excitement, had now returned with greater intensity, and as he ran he shut his eyes tightly, fighting back the wave of dizziness which threatened him.

'I must have been barmy to leave the bus as close as this,' he thought. 'She's probably been blown sky-high by this time.'

There was reason for his disquietude, for the enemy shells were falling uncomfortably near the field where he had left the machine.

But the Camel was intact when he reached it, although the ploughed-up ground which he had looked upon as a possible take-off, showed how narrowly some of the shells had missed it.

Biggles scrambled into the cockpit and revved up the engine, then kicked hard at the rudder-bar to avoid the

129

edge of a shell-hole as the machine lurched forward. Bumping and swaying on the torn ground, the Camel gathered speed.

'I'll have the undercarriage collapsing if I can't get off soon,' Biggles muttered, and eased back the joystick. For a few moments the wheels jolted on the rough earth, then a bump bigger than usual threw them into the air.

As he landed at Maranique, Wat Tyler, the recording officer, handed him a signal.

'From Wing,' he said. 'What have you been up to now?'

Biggles tore the envelope open and smiled as he read: 'Good work, Sherlock!' The initials below were Colonel Raymond's.

Chapter 9
The Great Arena

Biggles looked up from the chock* on which he sat while he filled a cartridge belt, carefully inspecting and testing each round for the slightest flaw, and throwing it out unless he was entirely satisfied.

'Haven't you finished yet, Flight?' he asked the flight-sergeant, who with a squad of oil-smeared mechanics, was working on the engine of his Camel plane.

'Five minutes and she'll be ready, sir,' announced the flight-sergeant.

'Well, get a move on, or it will be dark, and I want to test her to-night. I have to be in the air early in the morning.'

'Very good, sir,' answered the sergeant.

Biggles resumed his task. His face was tired and worn, for what with the big 'push' recently launched, and the arrival of the German Fokker D.VII's on the opposite side of the Lines, air activity had reached its zenith, and the British squadrons were not having things all their own way.

Replacements were slow in coming, for casualties had advanced by leaps and bounds until they reached a point far beyond the supply of new pilots, with the consequence that every available pilot along the Lines was putting in more flying hours than was normal. In

---

* Wooden block placed in front of an aircraft's wheels to prevent it moving before it is meant to.

131

common with the other pilots of his own and neighbouring squadrons, Biggles was feeling the strain, and there were moments when he loathed the war and everything concerned with it with a wholehearted hatred.

All he wanted was rest—from the first streak of dawn until the last rays of the sun he had led his flight on offensive patrols,* pausing only to rest while the fuel tanks were refuelled.

He longed for rain to provide a real excuse to rest awhile. The rain had come, but there had been no rest—the authorities had seen to that! And now, after having been in the air all day, his engine was having a badly-needed overhaul ready for the following day's work. Impatiently he was waiting for the mechanics to finish their task so that he could test it and go to bed.

'She's ready, sir, if you are,' announced the flight-sergeant, and the mechanics wheeled the Camel out of the hangar on to the tarmac. Biggles loaded his guns with the belts he had just filled, took his place in the cockpit, and after running the engine up to make sure she was giving her full revolutions, sped across the darkening aerodrome and into the air.

For some time he climbed steadily in wide circles, watching his revolution counter and air speed indicator closely. Satisfied with the machine's performance, he snuggled a little lower in the cockpit and glanced around him, finding a curious sort of rest in the lonely sky. Not another machine was in sight. The sun was setting in a dull red glow behind a mighty bank of cloud that was rolling up from the west. Below him the world

---

* Actively looking for enemy aircraft to attack.

132

was lost in a vast well of deep purple shadows, while the east was already wrapped in profound gloom.

Even the guns along the front were silent, for he could see none of the usual twinkling flashes of light that marked their bursting shells. It would seem that even they were war-weary and glad of an opportunity to rest.

Around, above, and below, was a scene of peace and unutterable loneliness. It was hard to believe that within a few miles thousands of men were entrenched, waiting for the coming of dawn to leap at each other's throats. War! He was sick of it, weary of flying, and the incredible folly of fighting men that he did not know.

Suddenly he started, as his eye fell on a tiny speck climbing up towards him out of the dim world below. It was a Fokker D.VII, a blue machine with a yellow tail, wearing the streamers of a flight commander. He wondered who it was and what sort of man crouched in the tiny cockpit of the enemy plane.

Biggles sighed, for he felt curiously tired and disinclined to fight. But he warmed his guns with a brisk burst of fire, and stood towards the newcomer with a queer smile on his lips. The Fokker made a quick dive for speed, followed by a zoom that brought him close, bright flecks of orange flame stabbing from the Spandau guns under his centre section. Biggles returned the fire, swung round behind the other, and in another moment they were racing round on the opposite side of a small circle, each machine in a vertical bank as it strove to get on the tail of the other.

For five minutes they flew thus, neither able to gain an advantage, although occasionally they managed to get in a short burst of fire. It was soon clear that the German pilot was an old hand at the game. Biggles,

133

beginning to grow dizzy with the strain, jerked the control-stick back in a lightning turn that gave him a fleeting chance to get in a shot.

A snarl of anger broke from his lips as his guns jammed at the crucial moment, and he hammered furiously at the cocking handles in a wild attempt to clear them, but in vain. In spite of his care, it looked as if bulged rounds of ammunition had found their way into the ammunition belts.

He glanced across the narrow circle at his opponent, now so close that he could see his face distinctly, noting with surprise that he wore neither helmet nor goggles. He was quite young, and clean-shaven, and smiling at Biggles' efforts to repair the jammed guns. Biggles could see every detail of the Fokker, even to the stitches in the canvas, and the maker's number.

And then a remarkable thing happened. The enemy pilot waved cheerfully, turned steeply, and before Biggles was aware of his intention, had lined up beside him.

The British pilot, half-suspecting a trick, watched him closely, but as the other made no aggressive move, the two birds of war flew side by side through the darkening sky. For some minutes they flew thus, smiling at each other across the void, and then the enemy pilot, with another wave that was half a salute, turned slowly and glided away towards his own Lines, now wrapped in darkest night. Biggles returned the signal and returned homewards.

'You're not a bad sort, Yellowtail,' he thought as he throttled back and plunged down into the misty depths. 'It isn't every German pilot who'll let up on you because your guns have jammed. You're a sportsman!'

134

Below him he made out the sheds and landing ground of his own aerodrome.

Colonel Raymond, of Wing Headquarters, Major Mullen, MacLaren and Mahoney were standing on the tarmac when Biggles landed.

'What have you been doing?' called the major. 'We thought you'd only gone for a test flight, but you've been away more than half an hour. We were just beginning to think you were not coming back.'

'Oh, just testing, sir!' replied Biggles abstractedly, for his mind was still running on the friendly behaviour of the yellow-tailed Boche machine.

'What! You didn't get those testing!' returned the major frowning, pointing to a row of neat holes in the fin of Biggles' Camel.

'No, sir. I had a little affair—nothing to speak of—with a lad in a yellow-tailed Fokker,' replied Biggles.

'Yellow tail, did you say?' exclaimed Colonel Raymond.

'Yes, sir. A blue D.VII with a sulphur-yellow tail.'

'They say Von Doering flies that machine,' went on the colonel.

'Shouldn't be surprised, sir,' Biggles observed. 'He certainly knew how to fly, anyway, and he's piling up a tidy score, by all accounts.'

'Yes, he is,' snapped the colonel. 'He's the man I've come to see you about! Let's go down to the office.

'It happens that I'm able to tell you how Von Doering is piling up his score,' went on the colonel, when they had settled themselves in the squadron office.

'If you had asked me I should have said it was because he's a better pilot than most people,' Biggles ventured.

'That may be so,' continued the colonel, 'but there is another reason. He has scored fast because, almost without exception, the men he has shot down had never before been engaged in combat!'

'Then he must be very lucky, or else he's a thought-reader,' suggested Biggles. 'How does he pick them out?'

'He doesn't—he's told where to find them,' returned the colonel. 'Now, listen. Von Doering has a circus of about thirty machines. As you know, it is now the practice for our new squadrons to be formed at home and then fly over here as complete units. Sometimes two squadrons come together, but in any case, they have to fly down the Lines, although a few miles over our side, of course, to reach the aerodrome they are to take over.

'About five weeks ago, No. 273 Squadron, flying Camels, flew over. Von Doering intercepted them and cut them to pieces. From all accounts, it was just plain massacre. Our fellows were shot down before they knew what it was all about. We thought it was a fluke until he repeated the performance a week later.

'He's done it four times now. He just happens to be on the spot every time when the new squadron comes along, and that's outside the bounds of coincidence. The Boche Intelligence Service is keeping him posted. There's no doubt of that.

'And so we are going to put a stop to Von Doering's little game. That astute gentleman is due for the shock of his life, and this is how it is going to be administered,' announced the colonel grimly. 'As you know, it has lately been the practice for squadrons to fly straight from their home stations in England to Marquise, just this side of the Channel.

'They spend the night there and then go on to their

136

new aerodrome the next day. It must be from Marquise that Von Doering is getting his information. The time that the squadron is to take the air has to be published in Orders—even if it wasn't, the officers concerned would be bound to talk about it, anyway—so the spy, as soon as he knows, sends word back to Germany, with the result that Von Doering is on the look-out for them.

'Now, this is the idea. To-morrow, 266 Squadron will fly to the coast, make a detour over the Channel and then land at Marquise as if they have just arrived from England. Officers will be warned not to talk about their war experience, and the pilots will have to behave as if they are all as green as grass and just over in France for the first time. Get the idea?'

'I get the idea about Von Doering attacking the squadron, thinking we are a raw lot,' admitted Biggles. 'But as we have only ten machines and Von Doering has thirty, it looks as if we've got a warm time coming!'

'Yes, you will probably have your work cut out,' Colonel Raymond agreed. 'You will fly at ten thousand feet, just behind the Lines, towards St Omer. It is near St Omer that Von Doering is most likely to attack. Have I made myself clear?'

'Perfectly,' replied Biggles in a voice that was not entirely free from sarcasm. 'Who is to lead the squadron?'

'I shall lead,' replied the C.O. 'A and B Flights, under Mahoney and MacLaren, will take position on my left and right. You, Bigglesworth, will bring C Flight along slightly above and behind.'

'Very good, sir,' was Biggles' only comment on the order which he realised quite well put him in what would certainly be the most dangerous place in the formation.

137

'Good! Then I'll be getting back,' concluded the colonel. 'Good-bye—and good luck.' Taking Major Mullen by the arm, he led him outside and whispered something the others could not hear. There was a faint smile on the major's face when he returned.

'We shall have to be moving early in the morning,' he announced, 'so we had better see about getting some sleep.'

Two days later, at six in the morning, the ten Camels of 266 Squadron stood ticking over on the tarmac at Marquise, waiting for the signal to take off. From the tiny cockpit of his machine, Biggles looked across at Algy on his left, and grinned. For the thirst for adventure was again upon him, and, as far as he was able to judge, the scheme had worked out so far exactly as it had been planned.

Experienced pilots all, they had arrived at Marquise the previous day, full of enthusiasm to 'see the Front,' and had lost no time in telling all and sundry that they were jolly glad to have left England for the theatre of war. It was obvious that all ranks, from the officer commanding the station downwards, were deceived by the ruse. Indeed, there was no reason why they should suspect the true state of affairs.

Biggles had had an anxious moment when a ferry pilot (whose job it was to take old machines back to England for reconditioning and bring back new machines to the Front) had asked him where he had got his M.C.*. But Biggles had passed the question off with a laugh, trusting that it would be mistaken for modesty.

Of the serious nature of the enterprise that now lay

* Military Cross, a medal.

138

before them he had no doubts. Von Doering and his men were seasoned warriors, and although their supposed victims were not likely to fall beneath the guns as easily as they might expect, the numerical odds in their favour was a factor that could not be overlooked.

Biggles wondered vaguely how many of the ten Camels now filling the air with the sickly smell of burnt castor oil,* would arrive at Maranique. But the roar of Major Mullen's engine brought him back to realities, and he sped across the aerodrome in the wake of the leader, bumping slightly in the slipstream caused by the machines in front.

'Well, here we go, with the stage all set for the big act,' he mused as the C.O., still climbing, struck off on their prearranged course. At ten thousand feet the ten machines levelled out and roared across the sky in the direction of St. Omer.

To the west, a few thin layers of cloud hung over the trenches, but in every other direction the sky was clear. They were now in their fighting formation. In front, the streamers on the C.O.'s machine fluttered in the breeze. Just behind him, and a trifle to the right, was Mahoney with the two other machines of his flight, while MacLaren with his machines occupied a similar position on the left.

With the wing-tips of Algy's and the Professor's Camels almost touching his own, Biggles brought up the rear, forming, as he knew quite well, the target upon which the expected attack would fall.

'The colonel must be crazy!' Biggles told himself savagely. For even taking into account the shortage of men and machines at the Front, which could only allow ten

* The rotary engine of the Camel used castor oil as a lubricant.

139

Camels for the job on hand, it was asking too much to expect them to counter the onslaught of a 'circus' like Von Doering's. But where the C.O. dared to lead, it was up to him to follow.

The late summer sun, now high in the sky, filled the air with shimmering rays that flashed on engine cowling, wings, and struts, making it almost impossible to see straight ahead without suffering temporary blindness. And from out of the blinding sun the attack would come. He knew that beyond all question, for Von Doering was too good a leader to overlook the value of such an asset, and he was in a position to choose the place and angle of his attack.

They were nearing the danger zone now. Biggles fidgeted in his seat, for, as in all such actions, the waiting was more nerve-racking than the actual engagement. From time to time he raised his fur-gauntleted hand, and squinted through the fingers at the blinding orb of the sun; but he could see nothing. Once a formation of British D.H.4's* passed below them, heading for the Lines, and the observers, coolly leaning against their gun-rings, waved them a greeting as they passed.

Where was Von Doering? They were in the heart of the danger zone now, and still there was no sign of a black-crossed machine. Had their plans miscarried? Had the spy been unable to get his message back—so that their flight to the coast and back would turn out to be nothing more than a joyride? It began to look like it, for St Omer now lay ahead, not more than ten miles away.

He raised his hand again and peered between thumb and finger, and caught his breath quickly. Could he see

* De Havilland 4, British two-seater day bomber 1917–1920.

140

something up there? Yes! Tiny white puffs of smoke—dozens of them. Archie—anti-aircraft gun-fire! White smoke meant that it was British archie, and that could only mean one thing—enemy aircraft! He half-shut his eyes and forced himself to peer into the dancing rays of the light that surrounded the gleaming white disc of the sun.

'There they are!' he muttered, as he caught a fleeting glimpse of a number of tiny black specks hanging in the air like midges. He glanced down quickly at the major's machine. Had the C.O. seen them? If so, he gave no sign.

Biggles rocked his wings slightly, raised his hand above his head, and looked quickly at Algy and then towards the Professor. They signalled that they, too, had seen the gathering storm.

He looked back at the major. What on earth was he doing? He had tilted his nose down slightly and was racing in the direction of St Omer, the other streaming along behind him. Biggles snarled. If Von Doering came down now and caught them in the rear, they all stood a good chance of being wiped out before they had time to fire a shot.

He lifted his eyes, and saw a dozen straight-winged machines dropping down on them like vultures. Something made him shift his gaze, and his lips set in a thin line as his eyes fell on ten more machines roaring down on their left flank. Seven or eight more were coming down on the opposite side. The sky was raining Huns!

He crouched a little lower in the cockpit, curled his lips back from his teeth in a mirthless grin, and shifted his grip on the control-stick so that his thumb rested on the gun-button. In that brief moment before the clash

141

he felt a pang of bitterness against the Higher Command that had sent them, like sheep, to be slaughtered.

Whang-g-g! Something smashed against the rear end of his port gun and richochetted away with a harsh metallic whir. A stream of tracer bullets flickered like a flash of lightning between his wings. Why didn't the major turn? Ah, he was going for them now! He had rocked his wings for an instant, and then zoomed up in a steep climbing turn. It was every man for himself!

Rat-tat-tat-tat-tat! Flack-flack-flack! Biggles thrust up his goggles and whirled round, eyes seeking his gunsights. As he turned, he caught a glimpse of two blue-painted wheels joined with a broad axle zooming up over his top plane. Another Fokker was standing on its nose as it roared down on his flank; he twisted to take it head-on, and sprayed it with a stream of tracer bullets.

The Fokker swerved wildly, and Biggles flung the Camel on its tail, guns stuttering vicious staccato bursts—rat-tat-tat-tat, rat-tat-tat-tat-tat! The black-crossed machine spun. Whether the pilot was hit, or merely throwing his machine out of the devastating stream of lead, Biggles did not know.

He had no time to watch it, but turned his attention to another machine that was diving on him with streaming bullets. He recognised it instantly. It was Yellowtail—Von Doering!

Biggles turned to meet it. His windscreen flew to pieces, and a blow like a whip-lash stung his cheek, but he did not flinch. At the last moment—only when collision seemed inevitable—Yellowtail swerved and the next instant they were tail-chasing in a crazy circle of wheeling, plunging machines.

A long, black plume of smoke through the middle

142

of the whirling dog-fight marked the track of a falling machine. A Camel was spinning to destruction, and two Fokkers, locked together, were turning over and over as they drifted earthwards, shedding a cloud of tangled wires and splintered struts. A flicker of flame licked along the side of the wreckage; one of the pilots stood up and leapt out into the void.

Where was Von Doering? Ah, there he was, coming at Biggles again! They missed collision by inches as they both turned and resumed their tail-chasing tactics. Biggles snatched his eyes away for an instant to look for the major's machine. Camels and Fokkers were scattered all over the sky in one of the most desperate dog-fights he had ever seen, but he could not see the C.O.'s Camel, and he turned back to Yellowtail, who was now trying to outclimb him.

Something bored its way into his engine with a thud, and a sickening smell of oil filled his nostrils. His engine revolutions began to fall. Von Doering, minus hat and goggles, swept past, slightly above him, and deliberately waved. He had recognised Biggles' machine. The British pilot waved back and jerked his plane's nose up to give him a burst of fire as he flashed across his sights.

Ah, what was that? Far up in the sky, in a line with the spouting muzzles of his guns, was a big cluster of black specks that rapidly grew larger. Farther above, another lot were dropping out of the blue sky like stones, and Biggles let out a wild yell as he recognised them. They were British S.E.5's, eighteen—twenty—no, twenty-four of them, and in a flash he understood the whole plot.

The S.E's had been waiting at St. Omer, far up in the blue—waiting for the Camels to lure Von Doering's circus to destruction.

143

'Jumping fish, what a trap!' muttered Biggles through his clenched teeth.

The S.E's were thundering down in formation, twenty-four blunt noses each surrounded by the halo of its flashing propeller, a never-to-be-forgotten sight! Von Doering was doomed, for he was too far over the wrong side of the Lines to hope to get back—unless he turned instantly, and he had not yet seen the British reinforcements! One or two of the others had, for they were diving full-out for the Lines.

The sight sent a curious wave of compassion surging over Biggles. It was all in the game, of course, this trap business, but it had also been in the game for Von Doering to shoot him down two nights ago, when he had him stone-cold with jammed guns. Without pausing to wonder why he did it, Biggles looked at Yellowtail, a hundred feet away on the opposite side of the circle, raised his arm, and pointed.

Von Doering looked back and up over his shoulder, and saw death in the streaming muzzles of the swarm of S.E.s, yet he waited to throw Biggles a gesture of thanks before whirling round and racing for the Lines. The S.E.s broke formation as each pilot picked out his man, although the enemy circus was now in full flight.

A Camel dashed across Biggles' line of vision. It was the C.O.'s machine, with the major waving the rally, and Biggles closed up behind him, looking round eagerly to see how many Camels were left.

One—two—three—four; another was coming towards him some distance away—five—two more were climbing up from below—seven.

Any more? No, seven was the lot. Three had gone.

Who were they? He looked to the right as Algy lined up beside him, pointing, thumb turned downwards.

'So the Professor's gone!' Biggles mused. Still, perhaps he had only had to force-land with a damaged engine. Four or five machines were smoking on the ground, but they were too far gone to be able to distinguish friend from foe.

One by one the remaining Camels fell into position, and Biggles picked out Mac and Mahoney, settling down on either side of the C.O. They, too, had escaped, then. And he fell to wondering how many of the enemy Fokkers would get back to safety.

With the advantage of height which British S.E.s held, it was impossible that the Boche planes would out-distance their attackers. They would have to fight every mile of the way back, with the odds piled heavily against them.

How many of the thirty machines of Von Doering's famous circus would limp back across the Lines? Two? Three? Not many could hope to escape the terrific onslaught of the British machines. There would be many empty hangars that night on the German side.

He breathed a deep sigh, for he knew the combat was over. Only the Camels remained. The other planes had vanished in the haze to the east. He sank a little lower in his cockpit as the major set a course for Maranique.

'I must have been crazy to give Von Doering that signal!' Biggles mused. 'I wonder what could have come over me? Still, one good turn deserves another, and we're quits now!'

145

Chapter 10
Biggles Finds His Feet

Cruising over the Somme, France, at fifteen thousand feet, Biggles paused for a moment in his unceasing scrutiny of the sky to glance downwards. The smoke from a burning farmhouse caught his eye, and a little frown of anxiety lined his forehead as he noticed that the smoke was rolling along the ground towards Germany at an angle which could only mean that a very high wind* was blowing.

He swung his Camel plane round in its own length, the frown deepening with anxiety as he realised for the first time that he was a good deal farther over the Lines than he imagined.

'It'll take me half an hour to get back against this wind. I must have been crazy to come so far over,' he thought as he pushed his joystick forward for more speed.

The archie bursts that had followed him on his outward passage with indifferent results now began to creep closer as the Camel offered a less fleeting target. The pilot was forced to change direction in order to avoid their unwelcome attentions.

'I must have been crazy,' he told himself again angrily, as he swerved to avoid a cluster of ominous

---

* Most First World War aircraft only flew between 70–140 miles per hour and a strong head wind would slow the aircraft equal to the speed of the wind.

black bubbles that had appeared like magic in front of him. 'I ought to have spotted that the wind had got up. But how was I to know it was going to blow a gale?'

Under the forward pressure of the joystick, his height had dropped to ten thousand feet by the time the white scars of the shell-torn trenches came into view. Suddenly he stiffened in his seat as a faint but unusual noise reached his ears. Underlying the rhythmic hum of his Bentley engine was a persistent tick-a-tack—tick-a-tack.

With a grim suspicion forming in his mind he glanced back over his shoulder. Along his line of flight, stretching away behind him like the wake of a ship, was a cloud of pale-blue smoke, and he knew then beyond doubt that his engine was giving trouble.

He turned quickly to his instrument board and confirmed it. The engine revolution counter had fallen to nearly half its normal revs. He looked over the side, now thoroughly alarmed, to judge his distance from the Lines. He decided, with a sigh of relief, that he might just reach them provided the trouble did not become worse.

But in this he was doomed to disappointment, for hardly had the thought crossed his mind than there was a loud explosion, a streamer of flame leapt backwards from the whirling rotary engine, and a smell of burning oil filled his nostrils. Instantly he throttled back, preferring to land behind the German Lines rather than be burnt to a cinder in the air.

He lost height rapidly, and fixed his eyes on the Lines in an agony of suspense. Fortunately, the sky was clear of enemy machines, a fact which afforded him some consolation, for he would have been in a hopeless position had he been attacked.

Still gliding, he moistened his lips, and tried opening the throttle a trifle. But the flames reappeared at once, and he had no alternative but to resume his former gliding angle.

The Lines were not much more than a mile away now, but his height was less than a thousand feet, a fact that was unpleasantly impressed upon him by the closeness of the anti-aircraft gun-fire. An ominous crackling, too, warned him that the enemy machine-gunners on the ground were also making good shooting at the struggling machine.

To make matters worse, there seemed to be a battle raging below. Clouds of smoke, stabbing spurts of flame, and leaping geysers of mud told a story of concentrated bombardment on both sides of the Lines. More than once the Camel rocked violently as a big projectile from the thundering howitzers hurtled by.

Biggles crouched a little lower in the cockpit, looking swiftly to left and right, hoping to ascertain his position. But he was now too low to distinguish anything except the churning inferno of smoke and mud. A battered tank, its nose pointing upwards like that of a sleeping lizard, loomed up before him and he kicked the rudder desperately to avoid it.

Barbed wire, tangled and twisted, was everywhere. Mud, water, and bodies in khaki and field-grey were the only other things he could see.

There was no question of choosing a place to land—everywhere was the same, so there was no choice. There came a deafening explosion, the Camel twisted into a sickening sideslip, and, with a crash of rending timbers, struck the upright post of some wire entanglements.

Biggles' next conscious recollection was of digging

148

feverishly in the mud under the side of his now upside-down machine in order to get clear, and then staring stupidly at the inferno raging about him. In which direction lay the British Lines? He had no idea, but the vicious rattle of a machine-gun from somewhere near at hand, and the shrill whang of bullets striking his machine, brought him back from his semi-stunned condition with a rush, and suggested the immediate need for cover.

About twenty yards away a huge shell-crater yawned invitingly, and he leapt towards it like a tiger. A bullet clutched at the sleeve of his coat as he plunged through the mud, and he took the last two yards in a wild leap. His foot caught on the serrated rim of the crater and he dived headlong into the stagnant pool of slime at the bottom. Scrambling out blindly, he slipped and fell heavily on something soft.

'Now, then, look where you're comin' to, can't you!' What's the 'urry?' snarled a Cockney voice.

Biggles blinked and wilted into a sitting position in the soft mud on the side of the hole. On the opposite side sat a Tommy, caked with mud from head to foot, a drab and sorry spectacle; upon his knee, from which he had cut away a portion of his trousers, was a red-stained bandage which he had evidently just finished tying.

'Was I in a hurry?' inquired Biggles blandly, regarding the apparition curiously. 'Well, I may have been,' he confessed. 'This isn't the sort of place to dawdle on an afternoon's stroll—at least, it didn't strike me like that. Where are we, and what's going on?' he asked, ducking instinctively as a shell landed just outside the crater with a dull whoosh.

'What did you want to land 'ere for? Ain't it bad

149

enough upstairs?' snorted the Tommy. 'Life won't be worth livin' 'ere in 'arf a minute, when they start puttin' the kybosh* on your aeroplane.'

'I didn't land here because I was pining to see you, so don't get that idea,' grinned Biggles. 'Where are we, that's what I want to know?'

'About in the middle, I should think,' growled the Tommy.

'Middle of what?' asked Biggles.

'The war, of course!' was the reply.

'Yes, I can see that,' admitted Biggles. 'But whereabouts are our troops, and where's the enemy?'

The soldier jerked his thumb over his shoulder and then jabbed it in the opposite direction.

'There and there, or they was last time I saw 'em, but they might be anywhere by now. You know, mate, my missus, she says to me, "Bert" she says – '

'Is your name Bert?' asked Biggles, to stop the long oration he could see was coming.

'Yes. Bert Smart, A Company, Twenty-third Londons,' replied the soldier.

'Nice name!' said Biggles.

'What's the matter with it?' growled the Tommy.

'Nothing! I said it was a nice name—nice and easy to remember!' protested Biggles.

'I thought you was pulling my leg!' growled Bert suspiciously.

'Oh, no, I wouldn't do that!' exclaimed Biggles, repressing a smile with difficulty. 'But what about getting out of here?'

'Well, I ain't stoppin' you, am I?' said Bert. 'If you don't like my blinkin' society – '

* Slang: finishing off.

'It isn't that!' broke in Biggles quickly, a broad grin on his face. 'I'd like to sit and chat to you all day—but not here!'

'Well, it's better than chargin' up and down, with people stabbin' at you, ain't it?' asked Bert. 'If you wants to go, there's a sap* just behind you what leads to our Lines.'

'A sap?' queried Biggles.

'Yes, sap!' said Bert. 'S-A-P—stuff what they put in trees—you know—trench, if you like. I wish I could come with you. Jerry'll be coming back in a minute, I espect. This is 'is property. We'd just driven 'em out when I copped this one in my knee and down I goes. Blighty** one, I 'opes. As my missus says, "Bert" she says—'

'Hold hard!' cried Biggles. 'Let's leave what she says till another day. Can you walk?'

'With no blinkin' knee-cap?' asked Bert. 'No! And I can't 'op neither, not in this muck! What do you think I am—a sparrer?'

'No. I can see you're no sparrow,' replied Biggles, looking at the man's thirteen-stone bulk. 'And I'm no Samson to carry you, much as I should like to. I'll nip across and tell our fellows you're here. Then we'll come and fetch you.'

'You'll fetch me?' repeated Bert.

'Yes,' said Biggles.

'No sprucing?' asked the wounded man.

'What's that?' asked Biggles, with a start.

'Kiddin'. I mean, do you mean it?' explained Bert.

'Of course I mean it!' replied Biggles.

---

* Communication trench.
** Slang: home, therefore a wound which would mean he was sent home.

151

'Well, you're a toff! All right, I'll wait 'ere!'

'That's right, don't run away!' grinned Biggles. 'Where's that sap you were talking about?'

'Straight over the top, about twenty yards 'arf left,' replied Bert, pointing.

Biggles peeped stealthily over the rim of the crater. In all directions stretched a wilderness of mud and water in which barbed wire, tin helmets, rifles, and ammunition boxes lay in hopeless confusion. A bullet flipped through the ooze not an inch from his face, and he bobbed down hurriedly. But he had seen the end of the shell-shattered trench.

Turning, he looked down at Bert, whose face had turned chalky-white, and Biggles knew that in spite of his casual pose the Tommy was badly wounded, and would soon die from loss of blood if medical aid was delayed.

'Stick it, Bert, I shan't be long!' he called, dragging off his coat and throwing it to the wounded man. 'Put that over you; it'll keep you warm.' Then he darted for the end of the trench.

A fusillade of shots and the chatter of a machine-gun greeted him as, crouching low, he staggered heavily through the clinging mud. Out of the trench, as he neared it, the point of a bayonet rose to meet him, but with a shrill yell of 'Look out!' he leapt aside and then flung himself into the trench.

At the last moment he saw an infantry colonel who was talking to another officer at the end of a communication trench. He did his best to avoid them, but his foot slipped on the greasy parapet, and like a thunderbolt he struck the Colonel in the small of the back. All three officers sprawled in the mud at the bottom of the trench.

The Colonel was up first. Jamming a mud-coated monocle into his left eye, he glared at Biggles furiously.

'Where the dickens have you come from?' he snarled.

'My Camel landed me in this mess,' complained Biggles bitterly.

The Colonel started violently.

'Camel?' he gasped. 'Have they brought up the Camel Corps?'

'That's right. That's why everyone's got the "hump"!' punned Biggles sarcastically. 'A Camel's an aeroplane in this war, not a dromedary!'

Further explanations were cut short by a shrill whistle and a cry of 'Here they come!'

'Who's coming?' cried Biggles anxiously to a burly sergeant who had sprung to the fire step and was firing his rifle rapidly.

'Father Christmas! Who do you think? 'Uns—the Prussian Guard—that's who!' snapped the N.C.O.*

'Huns! Give me a rifle, someone!' pleaded Biggles.

A bomb burst somewhere near at hand, filling the trench with a thick cloud of acrid yellow smoke, and he grabbed, gasping and choking, at a rifle that leaned against the rear wall of the trench. The din of war was in his ears—the incessant rattle of rifles, the vicious crackle of machine-guns, the dull roar of heavy artillery, and the stinging crack of hand-grenades. Near at hand someone was moaning softly.

Above the noise another voice was giving orders in a crisp parade-ground voice:

* Non-commissioned officer, e.g. a corporal or sergeant.

153

'Here they come, boys—take it steady—shoot low—pick your man!'

With his head whirling, Biggles clambered up the side of the trench, still grasping his mud-coated rifle.

'Hi! Where are you going, that man? Get down, you fool!' yelled a voice.

Biggles hesitated. From the parapet he could see a long straggling line of men with fixed bayonets approaching his position at a lumbering trot. Then a hand seized his ankle and jerked him back into the trench. He swung round and found himself staring into the frowning face of the Colonel, the monocle still gleaming in his eye.

'Who are you pulling about?' snarled the Camel pilot.

'What do you think you're doing?' grated the staff officer.

'I'm going to fetch Bert!' snapped Biggles.

The Colonel started.

'Bert! Bert who?' he asked.

'Bert, of the Twenty-third Londons,' replied Biggles. 'He's a pal of mine, and he's out somewhere in the middle by himself.'

'In the middle?' repeated the staff officer.

'Yes!' snapped Biggles. 'In the middle of the war, he says, and I reckon he's about right!'

'You're crazy!' said the Colonel. 'I can't bother about individuals—and I order you to stay where you are!'

'Order me!' stormed Biggles. 'Who do you think I am? I'm not one of your mob; I'm a flyer – '

'I don't care tuppence who you are!' replied the other. 'You're about as much good to me as a sick headache. I haven't time to argue. Another word from

154

you, and I'll put you under close arrest for insubordination under fire!'

Biggles choked, speechless, knowing in his heart that the senior officer was well within his rights.

An orderly tumbled into the trench and handed the Colonel a note. He read it swiftly, nodded, and then blew his whistle.

'A Company retire. B Company stand fast!' he ordered crisply. And then, turning to the sergeant: 'The Boche are in on both flanks,' he went on quickly. 'Get A Company back as fast as you can. B Company will have to cover them. And you'd better get back, too!' he snapped, turning to Biggles, who, a moment later, in spite of violent protests, found himself slipping and stumbling up a narrow, winding trench.

'But what about Bert?' he pleaded to the sergeant in front of him.

'Can't 'elp 'im. We're in the soup as it is!' snarled the N.C.O.

'The trouble about this foot-slogging game is the rotten visibility!' growled Biggles. 'It's worse than flying in clouds. No altitude, no room to move—no nothing! You blokes might call this a dog-fight, but I call it a blooming worm-fight! A lot of perishing rabbits, that's all you are, bobbing in and out of holes!'

His remarks were cut short by an explosion that filled the air with flying mud and half-buried him. He struggled to his feet, to see a white-faced orderly talking rapidly to the sergeant and point in rapid succession to each point of the compass.

'Surrounded, eh?' said the sergeant.

'What with?' asked Biggles breathlessly.

The sergeant eyed him scornfully.

'Mud!' he said. 'Mud and blood and 'Uns! You

155

ought to 'ave stayed upstairs, young feller. We're in the blinking cart, and no mistake. The 'Uns are coming in on both flanks!'

'But I'm due for another patrol at six!' protested Biggles, aghast.

'You'll be patrolling the Milky Way by that time, me lad!' growled the sergeant bitterly.

Biggles turned to the orderly.

'Are you a messenger?' he said.

'I'm a runner,' replied the lad.

'Well, let's see you do a bit of running!' snapped Biggles crisply, whipping out his notebook and writing rapidly. 'You run with that,' he went on, handing the orderly a note. 'Get through the Huns somehow, and don't stop for anyone. Grab the first motor-cyclist you see, and tell him it's urgent!'

'What's the big idea?' asked the sergeant, as the runner departed at the double.

'I'm just saying good-bye to all kind friends and relations,' grinned Biggles. 'Hallo, here's old glasshouse turned up again!'

The Colonel, followed by a line of dishevelled, mud-coated men, staggered wearily up the communication trench.

'Line the parapets both sides!' he shouted. 'We'll get as many of them as we can before they get us! Get that gun, someone,' he snapped, pointing to a Vickers gun which, with its crew dead behind it, pointed aimlessly into the sky. 'Is there a machine-gunner here?'

'I should say so!' cried Biggles joyfully.

He dragged the gun, with its heavy tripod, clear of the mud, and mounted it on the parapet. A line of grey-clad men in coal-scuttle steel helmets was advancing

156

stealthily up a nearby trench, and Biggles' lips parted in his famous fighting smile as he seized the spade-grips of the gun, thumbs seeking the trigger.

Rat-tat-tat-tat-tat! Rat-tat-tat-tat-tat! The grey line wilted and sagged.

'Fill some more belts for me!' shouted Biggles, ducking as a bullet cut through the loose flap of his flying-helmet.

'Here, stick that on your head!' cried the Colonel, passing him a steel helmet. 'Can you see anything?' he went on, crawling up beside him.

'I can,' replied Biggles shortly. 'Huns to the right of us, Huns to the left of us—and Huns blinking well above us! Look at that nosy parker!' he snarled, jerking his thumb upwards to where an Albatros had appeared like magic in the sky, guns spouting lead into their trench.

Biggles flung himself on his back and jerked the muzzle of the gun upwards. He knew what few infantrymen knew—the distance it is necessary to shoot in front of a rapidly-moving target in order to hit it. He aimed not at the machine, but well in front of it on its line of flight. He pressed the double thumb-piece. A stream of lead soared upwards.

The German pilot was either careless or a novice, for he did not trouble to alter his course in conditions where straight flying was almost suicidal. Straight into Biggles' line of fire he flew. The watchers in the trench saw the black-crossed machine swerve, and then, with engine roaring full on, plunge downward into the sea of mud. They could hear the crash above the noise of the battle.

'Got the blighter!' chuckled the sergeant. 'Good shooting, sir!'

157

'Oh, I hope he didn't land on top of poor old Bert!' gasped Biggles. 'He must have been mighty close. I can see his tail sticking up near my Camel. I wonder will that one count on my score?' he asked the Colonel. 'Although I don't suppose they'll believe it, anyway.'

'I'll confirm it,' said the Colonel vigorously. 'That is, if we get out alive. We're in a nasty hole!'

'So I see,' retorted Biggles, taking him literally. 'And I don't think much of it. I'm no mole. I like doing my fighting sitting down, and where I can see what's going on.'

'I'm afraid we haven't a hope,' went on the Colonel casually. 'The brigadier won't risk the brigade up here in broad daylight to get us out. We're for it, unless a miracle happens—and the day of miracles has passed.'

'Don't you be too sure about that,' returned Biggles, spraying a group of sprawling Boche with bullets. 'What about those?' he added, jerking his thumb upwards.

The Colonel cocked his eye towards a little cluster of black specks that had appeared high in the blue.

'What can they do?' he asked.

'Do? You watch 'em and see!' said Biggles. 'Give me a Very pistol*, so that I can fire a light to show them where we are.'

'Who are they?' asked the other.

'Friends of mine,' replied Biggles. 'I sent them word by a runner that their services were urgently required, and unless I'm very much mistaken, the boys in this trench are going to see a treat for tired eyes. That's

_____

* Special short-barrelled pistol for firing signalling flares of various colours.

158

Mahoney in front—you can spot his machine a mile off. And that's Mac over on the left.

'Oh!' he went on incredulously. 'What's all this coming behind them? A squadron of S.E.'s, with old Wilks leading! The C.O. must have 'phoned 287 Squadron after he got my message,' he grinned, and let out a shrill whoop of triumph.

'Here, we'd better bob down a bit, or we're likely to stop something,' he went on. 'I've an idea that this locality is going to be a pretty warm spot for the next few minutes when those lads start doing their stuff. Oh—look at that!'

'That' was a line of Camels that plunged down out of the blue and scoured the ground with double lines of glittering tracer bullets. Straight along the war-torn earth they roared, guns rattling, bullets thuttering a deadly tattoo on the ground. At the end of their dive the Camels soared upwards to let the S.E.'s go by, and then, after a steep, stalling turn, came down again, raking the earth with streams of lead. The Colonel watched in stupefied amazement. Biggles slid down the parapet and caught the sergeant by the sleeve.

'Now, sergeant,' he said tersely, 'I've got you out of a hole, and I want you to help me get someone else out of one.'

'You bet I will!' cried the N.C.O. delightedly.

'Come on, then!' cried Biggles, darting down the trench towards the old front line that had been their original position. Reaching it, he did not stop, but slithered across the intervening stretch of mud towards the crater near the crashed Camel.

Bullets zipped and whined about them, and Biggles had a fleeting glimpse of a grey-clad figure rising about thirty yards in front of him, one arm raised in the act of

159

throwing. Instinctively he flung himself full-length in the mud, dragging the sergeant with him. A moment later, a roar to their left, accompanied by a flame-hearted explosion, told them where a hand-grenade thrown by the German had struck.

Almost before the flurry of the explosion had subsided, Biggles was on his feet again, the sergeant following closely at his heels. Scrambling and slithering over the ground, they made a few more paces' headway. Then again that grey-clad figure rose up, and again the arm swung. But this time the grenade was not thrown. From somewhere behind them came the sharp crack of a rifle, and the German bomb-thrower sagged in mid-air in the very act of throwing.

It was the Britishers' chance—and they took it! Crouching low, they sped across to the crater where Bert was waiting, and scrambled down beside the wounded man.

Bert was sitting just as he had left him, calmly smoking a cigarette.

'Here you are!' he cried. 'I thought you'd gone without me. When I tell the missus about this she'll say, "Bert", she'll say – '

Biggles seized him unceremoniously by the scruff of the neck.

'Take his feet, sergeant,' he panted; and together they bore the wounded man to the rear.

They found the Colonel where they had left him.

'What are you up to?' he shouted, as Biggles and the sergeant came into view with their burden. 'I've been waiting for you. Couldn't make out where you'd disappeared to. The machines have opened up the communication trenches, and we can get through now. We'd better be going.'

Half an hour later, Biggles was washing the grime of war from his face in a headquarters dug-out behind the support trenches. The Brass Hat, monocle still in place, was talking.

'It was jolly smart of you to hold up the Boche advance by conjuring up those machines,' he said.

'Boche advance? I didn't know they were advancing,' replied Biggles. 'All directions looked alike to me.'

'Then what on earth did you do it for?' cried the Colonel.

'So that I could go and fetch Bert. What else do you think? I promised him I would, so I had to,' replied Biggles, grinning broadly.

Chapter 11
The Dragon's Lair

The Professor touched his rudder-bar lightly with his right foot and swung outward from the leading machine of the formation in which he was flying, and which had banked steeply and unexpectedly—too unexpectedly for good formation flying.

At the same time he took a swift, anxious look around the sky for the cause of his leader's sudden manoeuvre. It was unlike Biggles—who was leading a formation of three on an offensive patrol—to make a movement which might easily have resulted in a collision, had he—the Professor—been less alert.

Fortunately, his eyes had been glued on the leading machine, so the danger was averted almost as quickly as it had arisen. Unable to discover the cause of the quick turn, yet knowing that Biggles would not make such a move unless there was an urgent reason for it, he stared hard at Biggles' leather-covered head for a sign or signal.

Biggles must have sensed the penetrating stare at the back of his head, for he half-glanced over his shoulder and then pointed upwards. The Professor, after a quick glance at Algy, who was flying on his left, to make sure they were a safe distance apart, followed the outstretched finger with his eyes.

An aeroplane, a British Bristol Fighter, was spinning earthwards a few miles to the east, leaving a trail of smoke in its wake. Instinctively the Professor's eyes lifted, seeking the cause of the disaster. But except for a filmy white cloud drifting slowly across it, the sky was unbroken from horizon to horizon.

'That's queer!' he muttered, for he knew that things did not happen in the sky of France without reason—usually a very good one—and he returned his gaze to the Bristol, half-expecting to see the pilot make some effort to pull out of the spin. But no such thing happened.

A curious fascination held the Professor's horrified gaze, and his eyes followed the Bristol until it struck the earth with a crash that he almost fancied he could hear above the noise of his engine, about two miles behind the German Lines.

A cloud of smoke and a streamer of flame leapt upwards, and he turned away, sick at heart, to where Biggles was still probing the sky with his eyes, goggles pushed up, a puzzled expression on his face.

The Professor saw him lean over the side of his cockpit, sweep the ground with a long, penetrating stare, and then turn in the direction of the Line.

'Well, what did you make of that?' Biggles asked, after they had landed and removed their flying kit. 'I couldn't believe my eyes when he went right down like that, straight into the ground. There wasn't a Hun in the sky, and no archie, I'll swear to that. He was spinning when I first spotted him, at about six thousand feet, I should think. And there isn't a Hun machine in France that could have been so high in the sky that I couldn't have picked him out if he had been there!'

'Controls broke?' suggested the Professor.

'Broke—fiddlesticks!' snapped Biggles. 'That wouldn't set the machine on fire, would it?'

'More likely the gunner accidentally fired his Very pistol into his own cockpit, or into the gravity tank, and set the machine alight like that,' volunteered Algy.

'That might have been it,' admitted Biggles, frowning—'although it doesn't seem likely to me. All the same, I should feel inclined to let it go at that, but for one thing—or, rather, three things.

'Three crashes on the ground within a mile of the same spot! They were burnt out, so I couldn't say whether they were our own machines or Huns. But I've got a nasty feeling in my bones—only a feeling, mind you—that they were ours.

'I don't know what makes me think that, but there you are. There are four machines there now, piled up within an area of a mile. Why? That's what I want to know. It isn't the hunting-ground for any particular German circus. What did it, then? It looks like a new form of Hun devilment to me, and I feel like giving that place a wide berth. You'd better do the same. It isn't healthy. Well, come on; we'd better go and report the matter. "One of our machines failed to return," will be in the *communiqué* to-night.'

The mystery of the falling Bristol Fighter stuck in Biggles' mind all that night, and daybreak found him in his Camel plane, heading for the spot, drawn by some unaccountable fascination, almost against his will. He had never made any secret of the fact that anything to do with war-flying that he did not understand worried him, and this was no exception.

Why a Bristol should fall in flames out of a clear sky was a mystery for which he could find no satisfactory solution. Nevertheless, for his own peace of mind, it was

164

a problem he would have to solve before he could once more proceed on ordinary routine work.

He was approaching the suspicious area now, every nerve braced and taut. Unceasingly his eyes roved the early morning sky, clear, yet pregnant with a menace— a danger he could not define. He turned his eyes downwards and examined the ground closely, and he caught his breath sharply as he counted the number of crashes visible. There were five. Had he missed one when he had counted them yesterday? Had there been five crashes all the time? No, those circles of black-charred earth were too conspicuous to be overlooked. Another machine had 'gone west'!

His eyes lifted. Nothing above him. Eastward, toward the morning sun, they turned. Nothing there, either. What about the ground? A quick look revealed an apparently harmless French landscape—a few scattered hamlets, and the ruins of the once magnificent Château Contrableu, wantonly destroyed by vandals in the German advance, shining whitely in its park of verdant green. Even the roads were deserted. In the far distance a train was crawling along the Lille-Le Cateau railway, the only movement on the sleeping landscape.

Something—perhaps it was instinct—made him glance upwards, and simultaneously, so swiftly did his muscles respond to the will of his brain, he flung the Camel over in a wild turn that was neither a half-roll nor a bank, but an odd mixture of both. He had a fleeting glimpse of a dozen little white snake-like streamers of smoke missing his wing-tip by inches and then he was stunting as he had never stunted in his life before, all the time working his way towards the Lines.

A minute later he paused and snatched another upward glance. Only a small, fleecy cloud, too large for

165

an archie burst, broke the blue surface of the sky as it drifted sluggishly before the light breeze towards Germany. He hurried from the vicinity, still watching it closely, for a grim suspicion was already forming in his mind.

He recalled that there had been just such a cloud in the sky on the previous day, when the unlucky Bristol had fallen on the long drop to oblivion. He watched the cloud until it became no more than a filmy shadow, and finally dispersed in the light breeze. Then, in deep thought, he turned homewards.

'That was no cloud!' he told himself, as he landed and taxied in. 'Yet what could it have been?' No known form of archie could have made a burst of smoke that size—and what were those snake-like tendrils that left sinister trails in the air, like falling rocket-sticks? Where had they come from? What sort of machine had fired them?

He was aroused from his reverie by the urgent voice of Smyth, his flight-sergeant.

'How did this happen, sir?' Smyth was asking curiously.

Biggles leapt from the cockpit and hurried to the wing-tip which the N.C.O. was examining closely. A hole, about the size of a teacup, had been burned clean through the wing. It looked as if a red-hot iron had been placed on the plane and allowed to burn its way right through it, to fall out on the other side.

The flight-sergeant bent over it, sniffing.

'Matches!' he said. 'That's what it smells like to me—matches—the sort that have red tops!'

'You've got it!' exclaimed Biggles. 'That's it! Matches! Phosphorus! They're throwing up big masses of phosphorus, with an explosive charge inside to scat-

166

ter it! The charge bursts and sprays the stuff all over the sky, and whatever it falls on it burns. The piece that did that,' he went on, pointing to the hole, 'must have gone slap through without setting the fabric alight.

'Maybe it was because the wing-tip was travelling so fast—and I certainly was moving a bit—that the very speed put the flame out before it could catch hold. Flying's going to be a nice game if it starts raining phosphorus!'

'What are you going to do about it, sir?' asked the N.C.O.

'Do about it? There's only one thing to be done about it that I can see, and that is, find the instrument that shoots the stuff, and then put a lid on it—and the sooner it's done, the better! The idea of flying with lumps of red-hot phosphorus dropping down the back of my neck isn't my idea of aviation—not by a long shot!'

He found the other members of his flight having breakfast in the dining-room, impatiently awaiting his return.

'Well, have you found it?' inquired Algy, with his mouth full of toast.

'Not exactly,' Biggles replied. 'But I know what it is, so it can only be a question of time before we run the beast to earth.'

'Beast?'

'Yes—a dragon that spits fire and brimstone!'

'Dragon?'

'You heard what I said! Come and look at my wing if you don't believe it!' invited Biggles, snatching a quick cup of coffee.

'What are you going to do about it?' asked the Professor.

'That's what Smyth wanted to know. We've got to find its lair and then give it a dose of its own medicine!'

'Who's going to find it?' asked Algy.

'Ah, I thought you'd ask that!' said Biggles. 'The man who fancies his chance at it is likely to get the seat of his trousers warmed up. Our best chance would be to wait for a cloudy day—there's some cloud coming up now,' he added, turning towards the window.

'The weather report says wind high, south-east, fair at first, unsettled later. Thunder locally,' volunteered the Professor.

'Well, if we can find some good clouds to cover our approach, we may be able to snatch a quick glance or two. In that case we had better work independently, circling left so that we don't barge into each other.'

A few minutes later the three Camels were in the air, heading for the scene of action. Biggles, leading, was by no means satisfied with their plan, yet he could think of nothing better. Openly to approach the area where they had seen the unlucky Bristol fall flaming from the sky was obviously suicidal.

A close investigation could only be made at great risk. Yet how could they investigate without approaching close? That was the problem that baffled him as they drew near.

At his signal the three machines went off on different courses, each pilot employing any method he wished in an attempt to locate the machine or gun that dealt death so effectively. That it was a gun of some sort Biggles had no doubt, although it would have to be one of a large calibre to fire a charge heavy enough to form the huge white cloud that resulted from the burst.

'It might be a sort of mortar,' he reflected—'a large edition of those used by the infantry in the trenches.'

He glanced around at the sky. Great masses of dark rain-cloud were sweeping up from the south-east towards the place where the burnt-out crashes told their pitiful story, and he eyed the panorama moodily, uncertain how to commence his search. He saw the other two Camels, now some distance apart, disappear into a low surging belt of cloud, and then turned his attention to the ground.

For ten minutes he circled nervously, ready to act swiftly at an instant's notice, for this searching for an unknown antagonist was nerve-racking work. Not a mark, not a sign, not even the broad wheel-tracks of a gun-limber* or ammunition lorry showed anywhere to give him a clue as to the possible position of the dragon that spat a fire more devastating than those of legend or fairy tale!

Only the château, about three miles away, pathetic in its fallen glory, formed an outstanding landmark. He eyed it grimly. Nothing could have appeared more innocent. And yet, was there not something suspicious about its very innocence? Where were the troops that might reasonably be expected to have been billeted within those protecting walls? Where were the transport wagons, the horses of which could have been so comfortably stabled in those rambling outbuildings?

With suspicion growing in his mind, the place began to wear a more sinister aspect. Was this the lair of the monster? He did not know; neither could he think of any feasible plan to put his suspicions to the test. The

---

* Detachable front part of a gun-carriage consisting of wheels, axle and ammunition boxes.

idea of flying closer to it did not fill him with enthusiasm.

'Well,' he decided, 'whatever is to be done will have to be done soon.' For the clouds were thickening and dropping nearer to the ground, where he had no doubt they were precipitating their moist contents in the form of rain.

Where were the others? He glanced upwards, searching the atmosphere through a rift in the clouds. Then, without warning, from the opposite cloud-bank he saw something emerge. It was a sight so utterly unexpected that for a full minute he could only stare in amazement. Straight out of the swirling grey mist, sailing serenely across the open on a course that would take them immediately over the château, was a formation of eleven German Albatros scouts.

But that was not all; a formation of hostile scouts had long ago ceased to inspire him with either astonishment or alarm. Trailing along with the black-crossed machines, and not more than ten feet away from the rearmost, was a Camel. The spectacle of a lone British machine flying in a formation of Hun Scouts was so utterly grotesque that he was unable to make up his mind whether to laugh or be angry.

He saw, or rather he felt, the leader of the German machines mark him down, as he could hardly fail to do, and change direction towards him. And then he saw a sight that was to linger in his memory for all time.

The pilot of the rear German machine, seeing another machine near him out of the corner of his eye, turned his head casually to see who it was. Biggles saw him start violently as the other's amazed glance fell upon the flaunting red-white-and-blue cockade on the tail of the Camel. It almost seemed as if the Camel pilot

170

realised his mistake at the same moment, for there was a flurry of tracer bullets that brought half a dozen more Huns round in a flash, and the Camel shot into a cloud—like a minnow with a shoal of pike on his tail.

Biggles had a fleeting glimpse of the hopeless confusion into which the discovery had thrown the Boche pilots as they swerved wildly to avoid collision and then he, too, flung his Camel into the nearest cloud and dived in the direction of the Line. The prospect of getting mixed up with a crowd of Huns, or even British machines, for that matter, in the rain-cloud, was too risky to be lightly undertaken. He breathed a sigh of relief as he emerged once more into clear sky, and roared across the Line to safety, where he could give the unusual occurrence further thought.

Another Camel broke from the clouds a mile to the south, the pilot also racing towards his own country and safety. Presently a third emerged, the pilot streaking for Maranique as if intent on reaching home in the shortest possible time.

Biggles joined the nearest machine, and recognised Algy, laughing hysterically, in the other cockpit. Side by side they followed the homeward-bound Camel towards the aerodrome.

Landing, they taxied in, to find the Professor waiting for them on the tarmac. His face was rather pale from shock, or excitement, and he made no attempt to conceal either sensation as he unfolded his story.

'Are you tired of my company, or something?' inquired Biggles sarcastically. 'What's the idea—formating with a lot of Huns? Aren't we good enough for you?'

'Rats to you!' the Professor chuckled. 'If you'll shut up a minute I'll tell you what happened. I was circling

171

round, trying to spot the dragon, making the château the centre of the circle because I had a feeling that those walls were not so innocent as they looked.'

'I had the same idea,' Biggles said. 'Go on.'

'Well, every now and then I spotted you two at different points of the compass, and then I didn't see you for some time. But then I picked you up, as I thought, just disappearing into a cloud. I thought the best thing I could do was to close up behind you, because the weather was thickening fast, and I didn't want to lose you again.

'I figured it out that we would all emerge from the other side of the cloud together. So we did, if it comes to that. Only it wasn't you at all! The funny part about it was that I didn't spot any mistake for a bit. I noticed that we had come out of the cloud, and I could see some machines in front of me out of the corner of my eye, but I was really paying more attention to the ground. When I looked up I found I was in the middle of a circus of Huns.

'At first I couldn't believe it—thought I was dreaming. But when I realised it was true I got so completely shattered that I didn't know what to do, and that's a fact. Then I spotted that we were nearly over the top of the château, and it suddenly struck me that if I could throttle back a bit where the Huns might not notice me, I might get a close squint of the middle of the château. I reckoned that the gun, or whatever it is, daren't shoot while I was so close to the Huns, for fear of hitting its own people.'

'Pretty good!' grinned Biggles. 'Go on.'

'Well,' continued the Professor, 'the rear Hun spotted me just as we were passing over the building and I'll never forget the look on his face as long as I live. His eyes popped out so far that they nearly pushed his goggles off. When I saw that I was spotted I had to bolt for it, of course.'

'So I saw,' grinned Biggles.

'Yes,' went on the Professor, 'I bolted, and I don't mind, because I'd spotted it.'

'Spotted what?' asked Biggles.

'The dragon!' was the reply.

'You saw it?' cried Biggles and Algy together.

'Well, I can't exactly say I saw it,' admitted the Professor, 'but I saw all I needed to see. The middle part of the building is hollow. It's all scooped out like the cone of a volcano, giving a clear view upwards to the people inside. I saw them, all clustered round a big black thing. When they saw me they started dragging a canvas curtain across the top—but they weren't quick enough.

'When I looked back, the curtain was in place, and it looked like a roof—the prettiest bit of camouflage I ever saw in my life. Well, it's there. The question is now, what are we going to do about it? Who fancies his chance as St George?'

'We shall have to act pretty quickly now they know it's been spotted, or they'll move the thing,' declared Biggles. 'But it's no use being in such a hurry that we bite off more than we can chew. The man who flies over the top of that dragon's lair, or anywhere near the top of it, is likely to get a brace of dragon's eggs in his eye. We know that only too well. Wait a minute—let me think. I've got it!' he went on. 'We'll blind the beast first.'

'Blind it? How?' cried Algy.

'Smoke! We'll give it a dose of its own medicine. Now, this is my idea, and if anyone can think of a better plan, cough it up. Two of us will get a load of those

173

smoke-bombs the infantry use—there should be plenty of them at the nearest depot. We'll get well on the windward side, and lay 'em good and thick, keeping pretty low outside the arc of fire of the dragon.

'The wind will carry the smoke over the château so that the gunners won't be able to see a blessed thing. The third man then nips in and drops a bunch of Cooper bombs in the middle of it. If he scores a hit, the place should go up like an ammunition dump, with all those phosphorus bombs they must have got tucked away inside there. You found the beast, Professor, so—do you want to do the bombing?'

'Do I! I should say I do!' said the Professor.

'Good enough, then,' rejoined Biggles. 'Let's see about getting loaded up.'

It was nearly an hour later that the three Camels took off under the curious glances of the mechanics on the tarmac, and headed in the direction of the Château Contrableu. The Professor took the lead, with a neat row of eight Cooper bombs on the underside of his bottom planes.

Close behind came Biggles and Algy. On the floor of each of their cockpits, clear of the rudder-bar, reposed indigo-coloured boxes that had once contained rifle ammunition, but now overflowed with rags from the folds of which peeped the dull metal cases of smoke bombs.

The weather had become much worse as they roared along just below the thick moisture-laden clouds. The château loomed up, ghostlike, in the poor visibility, and the Professor, after a warning signal, swung away to the right.

The other two machines turned left, keeping some

174

distance to the windward side of the sinister building. The roar of their engines increased in volume as, with control-sticks thrust forward, they tore down towards the ground, levelling out only when they were skimming the tree-tops.

Biggles glanced over the left side of his cockpit to where Algy was watching him closely. He raised his hand, and then began to unload his bombs. A line of dense white plumes of smoke broke the dull green surface of the rain-soaked earth, and presently merged into a white opaque wall, which, under the impetus of the wind, swept across the ground and engulfed the evil château.

Like a single machine both pilots swept round in a steep climbing turn, and then tore back over the ground they had just covered, still unloading bombs. Then, still wing-tip to wing-tip, they turned their eyes towards the château and the solitary Camel now racing towards it from the opposite side.

Biggles, tense with excitement, saw the first Cooper bomb leave the rack, and fall short. The second dropped on the outbuildings and sent a cloud of debris soaring upwards. Then six bombs left the rack together, and his lips parted expectantly.

The next instant he was juggling with his controlstick as his Camel soared upwards like a rocket, as if thrust by a mighty invisible hand. His first impression was that his controls had jammed, and his second, as he realised that the Camel had only reacted to the effect of a mighty explosion, was that the Professor's machine must have been blown to atoms.

In the direction of the château a huge geyser of dense white and yellow smoke reached to the clouds, rolling and writhing like a colossal whirlpool from the force that had expelled it. Helpless, he could only watch. He saw the Professor's machine appear on the edge of the smoke, twisting and turning like an autumn leaf in a gale. Then it spun, levelled out, and spun again, obviously out of control. Two hundred feet above the ground it came out of the spin again, sideslipped steeply, missed a tree by inches, and then ran to a standstill in a long narrow field.

Biggles, with Algy in close attendance, raced for the spot, unable to understand what had happened, and undecided whether or not to risk a landing near the stricken machine. He had almost made up his mind to land when he saw the Professor raise himself up in his cockpit and wave. The machine remained motionless, the engine 'blipping' in sharp bursts. Then to Biggles' relief, it swung round, raced over the ground to the end of the field, and faced round into the wind ready to take off.

A line of grey-clad German troops appeared dimly through the mist, racing towards the field. Another line of them was surging up a narrow lane that led to the spot. Biggles turned the nose of his Camel towards the men in the lane, and Algy automatically turned his attention to the others. Glittering tracer bullets, starting from the noses of the Camels, cut white pencil lines through the grey atmosphere, and ended amongst the running German troops.

The Camel on the ground raced across the field and then soared unsteadily into the air. Biggles whirled round to follow it, and Algy brought up the rear. In Indian file the three machines dashed across the Lines.

'Are you all right?' yelled Biggles breathlessly, after they had landed.

The Professor blinked at him from red-rimmed eyes.

'Of course I'm all right!' he said.

'Why "of course"? What did you want to go fooling about in that field for?' queried Biggles.

'I should have crashed if I hadn't,' replied the Professor simply. 'I was blind—that smoke was worse than poison gas. It was only by the greatest effort that I managed to pull out in time to land. When I hit the dragon—or, rather, its bombs—I missed the main blast of the explosion; I had passed over it, I suppose, at the speed I was travelling. But I couldn't get clear of the smoke. It stung my eyes like fury, and then they just packed up so that I couldn't open them.'

'You must have got 'em full of dragon's blood,' grinned Biggles. 'Still, you've put him to sleep for good. Come on, St George, it's time we had some grub!'

Chapter 12
Biggles' Day Off

Eighteen thousand feet above the tangled maze of trenches that marked the greatest battlefield the world has ever known, Captain Bigglesworth, of 266 Squadron, throttled back to glide down to a lower altitude, for the early autumn morning air was chilly.

He turned slowly westward, searching each point of the compass as he turned, but as far as he could see the sky was empty. A frown settled on his face, for his nerves were straining under inactivity, and he longed for action to relieve the tension.

For a week he had scoured the sky, sometimes with his Flight, sometimes alone. But there was no enemy air activity in the sector—and he knew the reason, for a German prisoner had told the British authorities. Some of the German planes had been sent back to Germany with the task of harassing the British long-distance bomber squadrons of the Independent Air Force* who were daily raiding the Rhine towns, and others were concentrating south of the Somme, where the clouds of a great offensive were fast gathering.

The atmosphere was exceptionally clear, for it was one of those rare days with everything sharply defined, as if seen through the reverse end of a telescope. In the

---

* The bombing arm of the newly-formed Royal Air Force (RAF), whose task was to bomb targets on German territory. W. E. Johns flew with the IAF with 55 Squadron.

middle distance was the coast of France, with the English Channel stretching away beyond to a long, dark-blue belt on the far horizon that he knew was England.

'Kent!' Unconsciously his lips formed the words, and, following his train of thought, Biggles wondered what his old godfather, the eccentric Dr Duvency, was doing, for he had neither seen nor heard of him since the day he enlisted.

'I wonder if he is still there, or if he has moved inland?' he mused, for the learned doctor's home was not far from Dover, and German raids on south-east England, by aeroplane and submarine, were by no means uncommon. 'One of these days I'll fly over and look the old chap up!'

'Why not to-day?' The thought gave him a mild shock, for when it came to hard facts, he knew that such a step was very irregular, and would be unpardonable if trouble resulted from his absence. But, after all, he could be back before dark, and no one would be likely to miss him. The squadron would think he had dropped in for lunch at another aerodrome.

Slowly the nose of his Camel plane swung round under the gentle pressure of his foot on the rudder-bar, until it was pointing directly at the dim shadow on the skyline. In twenty minutes he was over the French coast, standing out to sea, with the chalk cliffs of Kent shining whitely.

Away to his left, a leave-boat was racing from Calais to Dover, leaving a white, zig-zag trail to mark its course, for, like all ships in waters where enemy submarines were known to be lurking, it sought to baffle the hidden menace by frequent changes of course. The ocean, as far as he could see, was dotted with smaller

179

craft, some obviously mine-sweepers, working in twos and threes as they dragged their nets unceasingly to and fro.

In the distance, a huge convoy of freighters was steaming up the English Channel, surrounded by a flotilla of protecting destroyers that sped through the water like greyhounds towards every suspicious object.

A great, dark-winged Handley-Page* night bomber, eight thousand feet below him, was making for Marquillies, on the French coast, guided by a 'ferry' pilot. From his superior height, it looked like a deformed water-spider skimming over the surface of the sea.

The English coast rapidly became clearer, and he could see the fields, woods, hedges, and streams that lay beyond, dotted here and there with villages. He set his nose towards a small village not far from Walmer, where the doctor's house was situated amid a smiling countryside of hopfields and oasts. He glided down steeply, then zoomed over the roof of the old manor house with a roar. Half-rolling on the top of his zoom, he swept down again, turned, then side-slipped neatly into a long meadow that bordered the orchard.

As the Camel ran to a stop over the rough surface of the field, he pushed up his goggles and swung his legs over the side, waving cheerfully at an amazed labourer who had been trimming the hedge, and who now stood, with his shears open in the action of cutting a twig, a picture of comical surprise.

A maidservant came round a corner at the double, followed by the gardener, the gardener's boy, and a pack of terriers. A shout came from the direction of the

---

* Twin-engined biplane bomber HP100. Carried approximately 3000lb of bombs.

180

garden, and next minute an elderly man in shirtsleeves, with a hammer in one hand and a chisel in the other, burst through the hedge and joined the others streaming towards the stationary plane.

'Hallo, there! Hallo, there!' he called as he ran, brandishing his tools. 'Hallo, there, young man! What's wrong, eh, what's wrong?'

'Nothing's wrong, sir,' replied Biggles, laughing at the old man's excitement. 'I've just slipped over to look you up, that's all.'

At the sound of his voice the doctor stopped dead, staring.

'Well, well, if it isn't young Biggles! Bless my soul, if it isn't! What brings you here, eh, what brings you here?'

'I've just dropped in to see how you are getting along, with a war on!' answered Biggles. 'I was doing a patrol over in France, and suddenly decided to slip across and see you.'

'You couldn't have come at a better moment!' declared the old man enthusiastically. 'You're the very man I want to see. The very man! Only yesterday I said to Bilkins, "if only young Master Bigglesworth was here, we'd soon end this war!" Didn't I, Bilkins?' he added, turning to the gardener for confirmation.

'You did, sir!' replied Bilkins dutifully.

'End the war!' cried Biggles, sliding down to the ground, 'how are you going to do that? I've been doing my best for some time, but as far as I can see I don't seem to have made much impression on it!' he grinned.

'I'll show you,' said the doctor quickly. 'Come with me, and I'll show you!'

181

'Still inventing things?' inquired Biggles, as they made their way towards the house.

'Inventing! I should think I am,' replied the doctor. 'A bomb!' he whispered. 'But not a word! If the Germans got an inkling of my self-expanding horizontal-action anti-submarine bomb, the place would be alive with spies!'

'What do the authorities say about it?' asked Biggles, with a straight face, although inwardly he was bubbling with suppressed mirth.

'Bah! What do they know about bombs? Nothing! Less than nothing! They say that my letter is receiving attention—and that's all it will get if I know anything about 'em! What they need is a demonstration, and what I need is a demonstrator. I am preparing to demonstrate it myself.

'I'm going to drop this bomb on something—a German submarine, if possible—if it's the last thing I ever do. And let me tell you that when this bomb goes off, it will make such a hole in the North Sea that the fish won't know whether they're coming or going. If it drops within a hundred yards of a U-boat*, the bits will be scattered from Heligoland to Harwich, you mark my words!'

'But how are you going to drop it?' asked Biggles.

'Come in here, and I'll show you,' answered the old man. They had reached the end of the field, where a large wooden shed, with a corrugated iron roof, had been erected, and he took a key from his pocket, unlocked a massive padlock, and swung the door open. 'What do you think of that?' he cried triumphantly.

Biggles started violently as his eyes fell on an ancient

* German submarine.

182

Farman aeroplane standing in the shadows of the impoverished hangar.

'What on earth do you think you are going to do with that thing?' he asked slowly.

'Fly it, of course!' retorted the old man.

'Where the dickens did you find it?' Biggles asked.

'Find it, indeed! I built it!' the other exclaimed. 'Built it out of scrap I obtained for experimental purposes!'

'It looks like it!' said Biggles. 'You won't mind my mentioning it, but it doesn't look like a very safe conveyance to me!'

'It doesn't matter what it looks like. It's the performance that counts. I've increased the factors of safety by one hundred per cent. You see, I'm going to fly it myself.'

Biggles started as if he had been stung by a hornet.

'You're going to fly it?' he gasped incredulously. 'When did you learn to fly?'

'I didn't—I mean, I haven't,' admitted the doctor. 'But I have studied the subject sufficiently to try my hand. I think I should be quite safe in the air.'

'As long as you stop at thinking, all right,' replied Biggles. 'But you mustn't ever start that engine up! Where is the bomb?'

'Here, under the nacelle*,' replied the doctor, looking a trifle crestfallen. All you have to do is pull this handle'—he seized a metal lever that projected from the fuselage, near the cockpit—'and the bomb drops straight off and explodes at the slightest contact. It has an instantaneous fuse.'

Biggles stepped back hastily.

* The crew section placed on or between the wings.

183

'For goodness' sake, let go of that thing!' he said sharply. 'Have you fitted any safety devices?'

'Safety devices? What on earth do you want safety devices for? A bomb is an instrument of destruction, not preservation!'

'Yes, I know. But you can't beetle around with a horror like that just tagged on to your kite. The thing might come unstuck at any moment!'

'For a fighting pilot, you seem singularly apprehensive of danger!' snorted the doctor, nettled.

'I'm frightened to death of that thing, if that's what you mean!' admitted Biggles coldly. 'If ever I saw a death trap, that's it! When I commit suicide, I'm going to do it cleanly, and leave something for people to bury in a wooden coffin, not scatter bits of meat and hair all over the landscape for someone to collect in a sandbag!'

'Very well, if you won't fly it, I will!' cried the doctor angrily. 'I've confidence in my inventions, if you haven't. Stand aside!'

'What are you going to do?' cried Biggles, seeing the doctor was in earnest.

'Fly it, man! Fly it, and put you to shame!'

'I'm hanged if you do!' snapped Biggles. 'Why, you'd never get it off the ground! Here, you get out of the way and let me have a go! I'll fly it for you—that is, if it will hold together long enough,' he added, in an undertone. 'And for goodness' sake take your hand off that bomb-toggle! Now, where do you want the thing dropped?'

'In the sea, off Dover!' was the cool reply. 'I'll ring up the harbour-master and tell him to watch the explosion!'

'If it falls off before I get there, he'll know I'm about without you telling him!' observed Biggles. 'I wish I could get the confounded bomb on my Camel, but the bomb-racks aren't made to carry things like that!'

Together they pulled the machine out of its shed, and turned its nose into the slight breeze. Biggles juggled with the throttle, then hurried round to the propeller. To his utter and complete amazement, it started immediately, although the rattle of the low-powered Anzani engine was not calculated to inspire confidence. He climbed up into the pilot's seat and tested the controls anxiously, noting with further surprise that they seemed to function satisfactorily.

'Off you go!' cried the doctor impatiently. 'I'll ring up Dover and then follow in my car to watch the bang.'

'I see!' replied Biggles. 'We shall probably go off together, me and the bomb, when I open the throttle. You'd better stand well clear, then you'll be able to tell them at the inquest what happened!'

He opened the throttle slowly and taxied a few yards, mentally blaming the folly that had led him into such a hole. He had no confidence in the engine, less in the machine, and still less in the home-made bomb and its fittings. But it was too late to back out now.

'I'm crazy!' he told himself angrily. 'Stark, staring, raving barmy, and all to please a daft, nit-witted old idiot with a bee in his bonnet! Well, let's get it over!' he thought grimly, and shoved the throttle wide open.

He turned pale as the wheezing of the engine swelled to a hoarse, bellowing clatter, and the machine lumbered heavily across the short grass.

'She'll fall to bits before she leaves the ground,' was his swift mental note during the next few agonising seconds, as he eased the control-stick back. Then he

185

breathed a heart-felt sigh of relief as the home-made aircraft rose sturdily into the air.

He circled slowly round the meadow, climbing for height, and, the immediate danger past, waved to the doctor and the little group of servants who were flourishing him good-bye on the lawn. Then he turned towards the sea, already visible in the near distance.

'I shall lose my commission over this business!' he muttered savagely. He crossed the coastline and stood out to sea—a precautionary measure which assured that if the bomb fell off its rack prematurely, it would fall in the water where it would do no harm—unless an unlucky ship happened to be in the way.

A naval flying-boat swerved from its course to take a closer look at the antiquated aircraft, the flying-boat pilot and observers making vulgar signs as it drew near, to indicate their opinion of the unusual spectacle. The flying-boat turned and dipped in mock salute as it continued its patrol, and Biggles swallowed hard with mortification, realising that it was impossible for him to overtake them to return the salute in his own fashion!

As he turned south, three Fairey seaplanes swept past him without taking the slightest notice, and the steadfastness of their purpose caused him to watch them closely. They were climbing fast. Lifting his gaze for a possible objective, Biggles ground his teeth with rage as he saw a line of white anti-aircraft gunfire bursts trailing across the sky, with a fleeting black speck at their head.

'A Hun raider!' he snarled, 'and here am I flying a dying cow! That's what comes of fooling about with lunatics. Serves me right. I'm flying Camels or nothing in future! Hallo—what's this coming?'

186

At first he could only see two players in a game which he could not understand. A little to his left, and a trifle below him, was one of those curious wartime small airships known as Blimps*, apparently steering an erratic course over an invisible switchback.

Almost immediately under it was the long, sleek form of a destroyer, most of the crew of which were staring upwards at the airship. From time to time both craft changed their courses suddenly, and presently it dawned upon the watching Camel pilot that they were acting in a sort of vague unison.

When the Blimp turned, the destroyer turned. But of the two, the surface craft was the faster in the face of the stiffish head-wind that had sprung up, and the antics of the Blimp were caused by the frantic efforts of its pilot to keep up with the other.

'Apparently I'm not the only one who plays the fool on the High Seas!' murmured Biggles, after watching this seemingly purposeless game for some moments. 'I suppose that's what's called fleet co-operation. I wish I had my Camel here—I'd show 'em a spot of co-operation!'

Then, quite by accident, he saw something else, something that brought a sharp hiss of understanding from his tightly-pursed lips. About two hundred yards in front of the destroyer, under the water, sped a long, grey, cigar-shaped shadow. That its crew were aware of the presence of its deadliest enemies above, was at once apparent by its desperate manoeuvring.

Being below the surface, it was, of course, invisible to the crew of the destroyer, and when it turned it

---

* A type of small non-rigid airship used for observation purposes—particularly naval operations.

187

temporarily eluded its pursuer, which over-ran it, and had to be brought back on its trail once more by the crew of the Blimp, who could see the tell-tale shadow all the time.

'A German U-boat, by all that's marvellous!' grunted Biggles, a quiver of excitement surging through him. 'It looks to me as if this is where I come in!' He turned flatly, for he dared not risk a steep bank in the crazy contraption he was flying, and sped along in the wake of the other three actors in this sinister game of follow-my-leader.

His heart came into his mouth as he struck the 'bump' of the Blimp's slipstream*. For a moment, he thought his controls had gone, but the next instant the machine was on even keel again, diving steeply under the gas-bag towards the destroyer. Just what the crew of the Blimp or the destroyer might think of his butting-in he did not know, nor did he care.

His eyes found and held the shadow of the under-water raider, towards which he was rushing at a speed that was likely to strip his wings off at any moment, although he was quite beyond caring about such matters in the excitement of the chase. Then his hand gripped the primitive bomb-release.

As he closed in, the shadow of the enemy submarine became less distinct, owing to his rapidly diminishing height, but he marked its course before it disappeared altogether. He passed low over the destroyer, and tore down to where he judged the quarry would be. Then, with a swift movement, he pulled the bomb-toggle, and

* The column of air driven to the rear by the propeller. Another aircraft flying through this disturbed air will have a rough or uneven flight.

188

jerked the control-stick back to zoom clear of the explosion.

Of the precise happenings of the next few minutes he had no knowledge, for his next conscious recollection was of swimming feebly in a sea of oil, trying to get his oil-corroded goggles off his face, and, at the same time, keep himself afloat. He was still only half-conscious when willing hands seized him by the collar and hauled him into a boat, where he lay gasping like a stranded fish.

'What were you carrying on that stick-and-wire chariot of yours—an arsenal?' asked the youthful skipper of the destroyer coldly, when Biggles had been dragged up on to the deck and more or less restored.

'What happened?' Biggles gasped.

'What happened? You thundering nearly blew us out of the water—that's what happened!' grinned the naval officer.

'But what happened to the doctor's kite—that's what I want to know,' asked Biggles anxiously. 'He thinks the world of it,' he added plaintively.

'Stand up and take a look,' invited the captain.

Biggles rose unsteadily to his feet, and staggered to the rail. The sea was thick with oil, in which pieces of wood and fabric told their own story. 'Is that all that's left of it?' he asked sorrowfully.

'I can't see any more of it, can you?' replied the skipper.

'No!' admitted Biggles. 'I can't! By the way, what happened to the sardine tin—the U-boat?'

'You opened it all right!—look at the oil! The thing you dropped would have opened a squadron of tanks. I've never heard such a bang in my life. What was it?'

189

'It was a patent bomb, made by a friend of mine!' replied Biggles. 'He asked me to try it out for him.'

'Well, you seem to have done that all right,' grinned the other. 'It was a pity he wasn't here to see it. Your kite just went to bits, like a busted egg, and you fell out of the middle like a newly-hatched chicken. Lucky you weren't high enough to hurt yourself!'

'Great Scott! How am I going to get back?' cried Biggles in dismay, suddenly realising his position. 'I'm supposed to be flying on patrol over Bapaume!'

'You'll be able to tell your old man that you did it over the North Sea, instead,' grinned the other.

'But where are you bound for?' demanded Biggles.

'Rosyth,' was the reply. 'Scotland, you know.'

'I'll get court martialled for this little jape!' muttered Biggles bitterly. 'I suppose there's no way I could get on that thing, is there?' he asked suddenly, pointing to the Blimp, which, with its engines idling, was hovering just above them. 'If the pilot's got a heart, he could put me ashore somewhere.

'All right, I'll signal to him to come down,' promised the naval officer. 'Those things can pretty well sit on the water when it's as calm as this. I could get him to put you ashore at Yarmouth—that's the nearest place he'll be able to manage.'

'Well, that would be better than Rosyth!' replied Biggles thankfully. 'I could get someone to fly me down from the station at Yarmouth to Manston, and that isn't far from where I left my Camel. I might still get back to my squadron before dark, after all!'

At four o'clock that afternoon a taxicab pulled up outside Dr Duvency's house and discharged a flying officer whose dishevelled appearance was certainly not in

190

accordance with the best traditions of the Service. His shrunken uniform had apparently been made for some-one several sizes smaller.

Biggles—for it was he—paid the driver, and hurried along a path that led round the back of the house towards the field where he had left his Camel. He had already opened the throttle preparatory to swinging the propeller, when his action was stayed by a peremptory shout.

'Hi! You there, what are you doing with that aero-plane?'

Biggles turned, and saw a dejected figure coming towards him.

'Why, hallo, doctor!' he cried. 'It's me, and I'm get-ting ready to buzz off; I shall have to put a jerk into it, too, or I shall be late.'

At the first sound of his voice, the doctor had pulled up short, then he came on at a sharp trot.

'But, my dear boy, they told me you had been killed!' he cried excitedly. 'Witnesses on shore distinctly state that they saw you fall into the sea after the explosion!'

'I fell into the sea right enough!' Biggles laughed. 'Look at my perishing uniform! It looks as if I'd pin-ched my kid brother's Sunday suit! They put it on the engine to dry, and shrunk the blinkin' thing to nothing!'

'Thank heavens you're all right! I've been nearly dis-tracted, thinking it was all my fault. Not even the Air Ministry telegram could cheer me up!' declared the old man.

'What telegram?' Biggles demanded.

'Why, don't you know? No, of course you don't! The captain of the destroyer made a signal to the Admiralty that a U-boat had been blown clean out of the water by an aircraft carrying a new type of bomb. The Admiralty

191

got in touch with the Air Ministry, and I have been requested to report to them to-morrow, bringing my plans and formula with me. I was going to call the explosive "Biggelite"—in your memory!'

'You dare, and I'll blow you and your works up with your own bombs!' retorted Biggles, coldly. 'I shan't hear the last of this, as it is; but if fellows in France were suddenly dished out with Biggelite bombs, my life would be a misery. You call it "Finalite"!'

'Why Finalite?' asked the doctor.

'Because it finishes things off—it nearly finished me off, anyway!' explained Biggles.

'Splendid! Finalite it is, then!' chuckled the old man.

'Good! That's that, then!' agreed Biggles. 'And you can send me a new uniform out of the profits. Well, I must be getting on, or I shan't be back before dark!'

It was a weary pilot who landed at Maranique that evening in the light of last rays of the setting sun. A little group of pilots who had been sitting disconsolately on the tarmac rushed to meet him, anxiety swiftly turned to hilarity when they saw who it was.

'Where have you been all day?' demanded Algy sternly. 'You've give us a rare fright. We've rung up every squadron along the Line for news of you, but you seemed to have just faded – ' His voice trailed away to silence as Biggles pushed up his goggles, disclosing two lovely black eyes.

'Where did you collect those?' asked one of the pilots.

'If I told you that I'd fallen out of an aeroplane over the North Sea and bashed my face on the periscope of a German submarine, you wouldn't believe me, would you?' said Biggles as he climbed stiffly from the cockpit. 'Well, I did, and I'm just going to make out my combat

192

report—'One U-boat shot down out of control and totally destroyed. Officially observed from shore.' That's more than any of you stick-in-the-muds can boast!'

Chapter 13
Scotland for Ever!

Biggles glanced at the watch on his instrument board impatiently.

'Another five minutes,' he mused, as he noted that the hands indicated five minutes to eight, the hour marking the end of his patrol. He glanced behind him to make sure that Algy and the Professor were still in their places, and then eased the nose of his Camel plane until it pointed in the direction of the British Lines.

He was glad when they came into view, for a leave pass—from France to Home—was in his tunic pocket, and although he was not superstitious, he had felt uneasy during the whole patrol. Somehow, he could not forget the fact that, for some unaccountable reason, ill-luck nearly always seemed to dog those who flew after that desirable document—a leave pass—had been issued.

Biggles had been surprised that his pass had been issued, for rumours were abroad of a great German offensive, which all the world knew, if it came off, would be a last mighty thrust at Calais and the last great battle of the war. The German plans were being laid with care. This time there would be no mistake!

Like a mighty battering-ram the German hordes would be flung against the hard-held British Lines, with what result no one could prophesy. All leave had been stopped for the infantry and the gunners, for the authorities had two important questions to answer:

194

Where and when would the attack be launched? They did not know, and they were taking no risks.

'Not for a day or two, anyhow, that's certain,' Biggles told himself, as he snuggled lower in his cockpit, for the March air was bitterly cold and found its way through the weak places in his well-worn flying-coat.

'Well, that's that!' he went on, with satisfaction, as he crossed the Lines and commenced a long glide towards the aerodrome. It struck him that there was a good deal of activity going on below, but he paid little heed to it, riveting his attention on the aerodrome which he could now see in the distance.

He reached for his Very pistol and fired the 'wash-out' signal, which meant that the patrol was over, and that the other two machines with him were at liberty to land independently. In answer to the signal, Algy and the Professor at once opened out and swung wide to allow their flight-commander to land first, as was usual, and Biggles began side-slipping steeply towards the hedge that marked the boundary of the aerodrome. At the last minute he levelled out, and the Camel bumped over the uneven ground, running to a stop at the very doors of the hangars.

The pilot breathed a sigh of relief, pushed up his goggles, and glanced upwards to see if the other two machines were coming in. Satisfied that they were just gliding in over the hedge, he turned and slid swiftly from his cockpit to the ground.

Almost before his feet touched the wet turf, he made a wild spring to regain his seat, but he was too late. Two pairs of grimy hands clutched both his arms simultaneously and dragged him back to the ground.

He stared unbelievingly into the faces of two grinning, mud-coated German soldiers—saw a crowd of

195

them beyond—then dropped his eyes to where the point of a bayonet was actually touching his tunic in the region of his stomach.

Subconsciously he heard the sudden bellow of the engines of the other two Camel planes, as Algy and the Professor discovered the situation at the last moment and tore wildly into the air again, followed by a fierce but futile hail of fire from the German troops.

To say that Biggles was stunned by the swift and incredible turn of events is to put it mildly. For a full minute—a long time for one accustomed to think and act with the speed of light—his brain reeled under the shock as he strove to grasp what had happened.

Slowly the staggering truth dawned upon him. The presence of the German troops on the aerodrome could mean only one thing. The great German attack had been launched while he was in the air. The British Line had been smashed, and the enemy was pressing forward with speed.

How rapid had been the advance, he could judge by the fact that the aerodrome presented its normal appearance. The sheds, the squadron office, and the officers' mess, as well as the air mechanics' quarters, were still intact—not destroyed as they certainly would have been had the C.O. received warning of what was happening.

Biggles did not know, of course, that the same thing had happened at several British aerodromes, and that the first notice many people had had of the big advance was the presence of grey-coated German troops, and Uhlans* charging across their aerodromes. Never was a

* Mounted cavalry troops.

196

retreat more sudden and overwhelming in its effect than that of the great Cambrai retreat of March, 1918.

Biggles realised instantly that something terrible had happened, and that the position of the Allies was critical. For himself, the affair was tragic, although even now the full enormity of the tragedy had not penetrated his numbed brain.

The Germans, who seemed to be in a good mood as a result of their victory, offered him no bodily harm, somewhat to his surprise. In fact, it was obvious at a glance that they themselves hardly knew what they were doing, so sudden and unexpected had been the break-through.

For the moment he had been left, exactly where he had dismounted, with an armed guard, and although he looked longingly at his Camel, so near and yet so far, he made no move towards it, for he knew beyond doubt that such an action would be suicidal. For the Germans would shoot on the slightest provocation—for which they could hardly be blamed—and at such a point-blank range it was asking for a miracle to expect them to miss him.

He decided swiftly that it was no earthly use just throwing his life away on the impulse of the moment. Sooner or later, a more reasonable opportunity to escape would present itself, and when that time came he would not be slow in taking advantage of it.

An orderly now appeared, and, after a few words in guttural German, the party moved off towards what that morning had been the squadron office of Squadron No. 266, R.F.C. Now, from the C.O.'s chair, a German officer regarded him coldly.

'So,' he said in quite good English, 'you have had bad luck!'

'You've said it in one,' Biggles agreed.

'Your name?' the officer demanded.

'Bigglesworth—most people call me Biggles for short,' he added, with a grin.

'Rank?'

'Captain.'

'Squadron?'

Biggles shook his head.

'That I must ask you to find out for yourself,' he said.

The German flushed.

'It will pay you to be accommodating!' he said harshly.

Biggles eyed him coolly.

'My name and rank I have told you, and that, as you know, is as much as I am compelled to tell you by the rules of war. In fairness to you, and in order to save you wasting your time, I may as well say at once that I have no intention of imparting any further information of any sort. In fairness to myself, I trust you will not ask me. Just think what you would do if the positions were reversed!'

The German looked at him with a curious expression on his face.

'Your friends were fortunate!' he observed. 'But for the fools outside showing themselves too soon, we should have captured three instead of one. Well, it makes little difference. For you, the war is over. Germany has broken your Line, and nothing can now stop our advance to Paris and to victory!'

'That may be so,' admitted Biggles, for, in the circumstances, the statement did not seem unreasonable; in any case, it was hardly worth contradicting.

'Well, your friends are gone – '

'But not forgotten,' interrupted Biggles, whose keen

198

ear had detected the distant sound of aero-engines. At the same time a pang of misgiving shot through him. Every step would be taken by the authorities to destroy the war material that had fallen into German hands, and if British squadrons were now returning to bomb the aerodrome, as he strongly suspected they were, he stood a fair chance of losing his life in the raid!

The German officer cocked his ear and listened. 'Our airmen are arriving!' he said triumphantly.

'Yes, our airmen are arriving,' agreed Biggles, not in the least surprised at the German's ignorance, for an infantryman could hardly be expected to tell the difference between the musical hum of the British Bentley engine and the deeper and more sinister growl of the German Benz or Mercedes.

Biggles knew without looking that the machines arriving were British Camels, not German Albatroses or Fokkers. Suddenly the notes of the engines increased in volume and there came a sound of rifle-fire from outside. A German non-commissioned officer burst into the room, frantic with excitement.

He started to say something, but the scream of a falling bomb drowned his words. Biggles, risking a thrust from a bayonet, flung himself flat on his face, and he was only just in time.

There was a deafening crash outside, another, and then the squadron office seemed to leap into the air from the centre. Biggles was on his feet in a moment, gasping and choking in a blue cloud of acrid smoke. One glance revealed the full havoc caused by the bomb.

The German officer lay motionless, half-buried under a pile of debris. The N.C.O. had completely disappeared, while the two guards were both struggling to rise, one groaning.

The room itself was completely wrecked. Maps and pictures had fallen from the walls, files of documents had been blown from their cases, strewing their contents over the splintered furniture.

Flicking a trickle of blood from his eyes, for his forehead had been grazed by a splinter, Biggles stepped quickly under the sagging doorway into the hall. As he expected, five or six flying-coats and helmets still hung from their pegs, just as they had been left by the departing officers of his squadron.

He slipped one of the coats on, jammed a helmet on his head, then hurried along the corridor to the rear of the building, where the crash of bursting bombs told him that the work of destruction was still being pursued with vigour.

Two German soldiers rushed past him, too taken up with their own safety to worry about him, or else they did not recognise him.

Reaching the door he paused for a moment, uncertain what to do next or which direction to take. In spite of his precarious position, a grin flickered across his face as he glanced upwards at the British scouts that were banking, wheeling, zooming, diving, and turning to dive again. The aerodrome was bedlam let loose, and the din terrific.

Yet, in spite of the bombardment, little damage of real importance had been done. True, his Camel lay a tangled and twisted wreck of torn fabric and splintered wood, and the two end hangars were blazing furiously, but the ammunition store and armoury were intact, as was the petrol dump.

After a brief survey of the scene, his first impulse was

200

the most natural one—it was to get an aeroplane and escape! Any aeroplane would do as long as it would fly, and with this intention in view he darted towards the nearest hangar.

Most of the Germans were busy seeking shelter, or firing at the Camels that were now raking the ground with streams of tracer bullets, and with his leather coat buttoned up, there was nothing to indicate that he was not a German pilot or dispatch-rider.

He reached the hangar, but had to fling himself flat as a Camel, with its wheels grazing the ground, bore down on him, its guns crackling. Glancing upwards as it passed over him he saw its number, and recognised Algy's machine.

'That's the stuff, boy!' he murmured approvingly. There was no possible means by which he could convey his identity to the pilot, who had passed over him at a speed that could not have been much less than a hundred and fifty miles an hour.

The immediate danger past, Biggles sprang to his feet and hurried into the hangar. To his bitter disappointment it was empty, except for half a dozen German soldiers skulking in a corner. They sprang to their feet, sheepishly, when they saw him, evidently mistaking him for a German officer. With a lordly wave of his arm that might have meant anything, he turned on his heel and ran round to the back of the hangar.

Which way? He knew the direction where the British troops would be, but he had no idea how far away they were. One thing was certain—in order to reach them he would have to pass through the German Lines that had moved forward with the attack.

Moreover, he had no doubt that a fierce battle was

raging in that direction, as the British strove to stem the tide and the Germans endeavoured to press home their advantage. To make his way through the barrage that would be forming by the time he reached the spot, without being hit by one side or the other, was asking for the impossible. So, for the first time in his life, he was absolutely nonplussed.

Presently the Camels would depart, when the Germans would recover their composure and start looking for their prisoner.

The only course that seemed open to him was to find a hiding-place where he could lie low until the tide of war surged over him, when it might be possible to devise some plan for reaching the nearest frontier.

That the aerodrome was lost was certain, and he eyed a stack of petrol cans that had escaped the raiders. He looked at the ammunition hut, where the squadron's bombs as well as machine-gun ammunition were stored. It was a pity it hadn't been destroyed, he reflected, for the Germans would soon be using it against them. Well, he would see what could be done about it.

The Camels were rallying now, obviously preparing to depart, so there was little time to lose. Behind him the sheds were still blazing. To his left, the mess and ante-room were still standing, although they had suffered considerably. German troops were everywhere, some lying down firing their rifles at the Camels, others gathered at certain points under the supervision of officers and N.C.O.s. None of them was paying any attention to him.

Suddenly making up his mind, he whipped up a can of petrol in each hand and walked briskly towards the ammunition store. He would prevent that falling into

German hands, anyway! The door, as he expected, was locked, but he put his shoulder to it and forced it open.

It was the work of a moment to unscrew the caps from the petrol tins and fling them inside, and throw a lighted match on the gurgling liquid that gushed out. So far so good, he thought, as he beat a hasty retreat.

Which way? He started off towards the village of Maranique, which would normally have been well behind the British Lines, but the appearance of a surging crowd of German troops, and the brisk rattle of rifle fire, caused him to change his mind and turn hurriedly towards the only available hiding-place—the ruins of the officers' mess.

He reached it without being challenged, and glanced inside. The German officer still lay where he had fallen, but his eyes were wide open, and on the appearance of his late prisoner his hand moved rapidly.

Biggles sprang sideways as the hand reappeared gripping a revolver, and a bullet buried itself in the wall. He stooped at the end of his jump, snatched up the loose leg of a chair, and without hesitation brought it down on the German's head.

'You hold that, and lie still for a bit!' he growled.

A sudden noise of shouting sent him swiftly to a window. Clouds of black smoke were streaming across the aerodrome from the burning ammunition hut, towards which a crowd of Germans were hurrying under the direction of an N.C.O., with the obvious intention of subduing the flames, if possible. From another direction a fresh crowd was converging upon the mess.

'I'm sunk!' Biggles muttered, looking around desperately. 'If they come in here I'm done for!' Only one place of concealment was open to him—a gaping hole in the ceiling, through which the bomb had crashed and demolished a large part of it, exposing a dark cavity between the ceiling of the room and the rafters of the sloping roof.

Without further delay he took a running jump, seized the edge of the ceiling—which rocked sickeningly in his grasp—then pulled himself into the recess.

He was not a moment too soon. Hardly had he wriggled along to the end wall, and stretched himself on the floor in the darkest place, than a party of Germans bundled into the building and took up positions at the windows.

At the same instant there was a terrific burst of rifle fire from somewhere near at hand, and it took him a minute or two to realise that it was the small arms ammunition exploding in the heat of the flames. A moment later there was a mighty roar as the ammunition hut blew up, and the air became black with fumes.

Almost stunned by the explosion and the clamour below, he lay still, wondering vaguely what would happen next. He was soon to know! There came a long, whinnying howl, followed immediately by a vicious plop!—and again the place rocked to the roar of an explosion. Then came another and another, until the air was filled with the shriek of shells, punctuated with explosions.

'It's the British guns!' groaned Biggles. 'They're shelling us now!' He could do nothing except remain where he was and hope for the best. 'What a war!' he muttered, half-sick with the din and anxiety. 'What a war!'

Then came more shouting from below, and rifle fire of such intensity that it brought a faint gleam of hope to his mind. The British were counter-attacking! If they could retake the aerodrome he would be saved!

The din in the room underneath became indescribable. And then his ear caught a sound that set his heart palpitating violently. He felt the roof sag as if under a heavy weight, and the next minute a German soldier hauled himself up into the cavity and lay flat, staring down into the room. Then came another, but they did not so much as glance in his direction.

They both lay flat and stretched their arms downwards for something that was being handed up to them below. The muzzle of a German maxim-gun* came into view, and then the whole weapon. The first German quickly hacked a hole through the soft felt roofing. The gun was dragged into position, and began spitting viciously.

From time to time a voice of authority from below shouted to the two men manipulating the gun, but Biggles had no idea what was said. Box after box of ammunition was handed up and worked through the gun, and presently the firing below decreased in volume.

For a few minutes Biggles struggled to understand what was going on, and then the solution burst upon him. The machine-gun was holding up the advance of the returning British troops!

'So that's it, is it!' he breathed. The knowledge that the gun was probably mowing down scores of British Tommies put a different complexion on matters; escape

* The name maxim originated from the inventor, the American Hiram Maxim, whose basic machine gun design was adopted by German and British manufacturers.

now became a matter of secondary consideration. At all costs the gun must be silenced, though Biggles knew quite well that he could not hope to fight the crowd surging in the ante-room.

Still, he might put the gun out of action for a few minutes, either by damaging it or by toppling it bodily through the hole into the room below.

The next instant he was wriggling like a snake towards the gunners, who, unconscious of their danger, were in the act of reloading. On his way his hand closed over a length of rafter that had been ripped off by the bomb, and he clung to it desperately.

He was on the gunners before they were aware of his presence. There was no room to wield the improvised club above his head, but he rose to his knees and swung it around horizontally, putting his full weight behind the blow.

The first gunner, as if warned by instinct, looked up at the precise moment that the weapon reached him. The rough edge caught him slap in the face and lifted him bodily through the hole as if he had been a feather cushion.

The force of the blow was such that the wood splintered in Biggles' grasp, leaving him clutching a jagged piece about two feet long. Before the second gunner had time to grasp what was happening, Biggles, using his weapon like a bayonet, prodded him violently in the pit of the stomach, and then, as the other doubled up, brought it down with a resounding whack on the back of the gunner's head.

The German collapsed limply across the gun, and Biggles, without further ado, kicked him through the hole, where he crashed to the floor, narrowly missing an

206

officer who had at that moment arrived to see what the unusual sounds meant.

Breathing heavily, Biggles paused in his work and stared straight down into the startled faces of a dozen German soldiers! With a gasp of exertion he sprang to the gun, dragged it from its temporary emplacement, and jerked the muzzle downwards.

For perhaps two seconds he fumbled with the unusual firing arrangements, while bullets tore and ripped through the flimsy woodwork around him; then his thumbs closed over the firing button and jabbed it viciously.

It is impossible to describe the scene of confusion that followed. Biggles, quite beside himself now that the fighting fever was upon him, traversed the floor from end to end in long bursts. Below, all was pandemonium, yells mingling with the crash of rifles and the ripping of woodwork.

Then came a sound that sent the blood surging to his head. It was a wild, ringing, British cheer.

As one man, the surviving Germans fled helter-skelter through the doorway, and Biggles sank limply across the gun as the line of troops in familiar British 'tin' helmets, khaki tunics, and kilts of a Scots regiment poured into the room, a sergeant at their head.

'Hey, sling a bomb in yon hole, Angus!' roared the sergeant. 'Some o' them may still be skulkin' aboot!'

Biggles, still dazed, saw a brawny Highlander whip out a black, egg-shaped thing from his pocket; his arm went back like a bowler's –

'Och hi! Hold hard!' yelled Biggles.

The effect of his words was comical. The sergeant's mouth gaped open and his eyes goggled in his head.

'Hoots, mon!' said a voice.

207

'Never mind hooting!' said Biggles. 'Help me down!'

An officer burst through the doorway, revolver in hand, but he stopped dead as his eyes fell on the smoke-blackened face peering down at him.

'Come on doon oot o' that!' he snapped fiercely. 'I want you!'

Biggles slid his legs over the edge of the ceiling until they were swinging in space.

'Is that so?' he said coolly. 'I'll ask you to remember that you're a guest in my mess—but I'm real glad to see you. Come right in! And it looks to me as if 'mess' is a good name for it, too!' he added, his eyes roving over the scene of destruction. 'My aunt, what a bloomin' mess!'

'Who are you?' asked the officer curiously, stepping forward.

'Name's Bigglesworth—they call me Biggles for short. This is my aerodrome, or what's left of it—or, at least, it was. The Germans nabbed me, but I got away.'

'Did you silence that gun up there?' asked the Highlander.

'I did,' replied Biggles. 'I had to do something about it. You see, I'm going on leave to-day, and I was afraid I should miss my train. Scotland for ever!'